Pra:

Untamed Hearts

Sizzling hot and emotionally satisfying, readers are sure to enjoy Wolfen Choice. ~ *Joyfully Reviewed*

These two have a sexual chemistry that required fireproofing your home. But, it's the emotions Zane draws from Cole that makes their relationship ascend from sexual to loving mates. I found Wolfen Choice to be an enjoyable read.
~ *Fallen Angel Reviews*

I love collaboration that works. Mason and Byrnes and has a style all their own that works well. Mason brings the angst and Byrnes brings the humanity - a brilliant combo. ~ *Erotic Horizon*

UNTAMED HEARTS
Volume Two

Wolfen Choice

Stallion's Pride

JENNA BYRNES
JUDE MASON

Untamed Hearts Volume Two
ISBN # 978-0-85715-065-3
©Copyright Jenna Byrnes and Jude Mason 2010
Cover Art by April Martinez ©Copyright 2010
Interior text design by Claire Siemaszkiewicz
Total-E-Bound Publishing

WOLFEN CHOICE

Dedication

To our loyal readers, here's hoping you feel like
Cole—young at heart, carefree, and always, the
chosen one

Chapter One

Cole sat with his back to the cliff face, naked as the day he was born. The rough stone scratched his back, the rubble under him dug into his bum. He focused on a distant point where flames had licked at the treetops, leaving nothing but blackened fingers reaching into the sky.

The fire had recently passed over the valley, leaving the territory of the wolf tribe a mixture of ashes and partially burnt foliage. If Gar hadn't been away from home, if the wind had turned the other way, Cole was sure life would have gone on as usual. Many of the small family packs had fought the flames, while others had fled. But without Gar, the pall of death now loomed over the entire tribe.

Cole's immediate thoughts were of his find and the meaning behind it. The talisman. The brilliant red stone in the shape of a wolf's head, set in the centre of the gold filigree, rested in his palm. He wanted to throw it as far as his strength would allow. Instead, he tossed it into the air and snatched it back then lifted it so the sun shone through the gem, sending brilliant shards of colour across the dull, burned soil.

"What's the matter?" Zane, his friend and companion, leaned down and, reaching out, tried to snatch the stone from his grasp.

Cole pulled the amulet close, unwilling to allow it to leave his hand. Cursing under his breath, he wondered why. He'd have given anything if he'd never seen the damn thing—never found their tribal leader, Gar, and his mate's scorched corpses. Charred flesh and bone had been all that remained. The smell was something he'd never forget, he was sure of it.

The shock and grief were still hard to bear. The ramifications of what this meant to their tribe were enormous. Cole sighed. No one would ever be able to replace Gar. Yet someone would have to try.

Shaking off his black mood, he dropped the amulet onto the pile of clothing he'd shed and grabbed hold of Zane's wrist. He pulled the tan-fleshed, white-haired man around and draped him across his knees. "Nothing besides the obvious," he said, answering Zane's question. "Oh, and I'm horny." It seemed inappropriate, but Cole needed something to distract him from the horrible events that had taken place.

Zane's response was predictable, as had been Cole's own comment. "Yeah, so what else is new? Ever since I met you, your cock's been at no less than half-hard."

"Nothing wrong with that, or so you've been telling me for the past couple of weeks. No one else complains about me being hard all the time."

Zane wriggled, dragging his thighs and genitals over Cole's erection. "Like I'm complaining!" He squirmed a little more and chuckled when Cole groaned.

"Fuck, you know how to get to me." Cole slid his hand over Zane's lower back then along his arse. The man's squirming took on a more determined thrust, driving his shaft hard into Cole's thigh.

"I understand how you're feeling. This whole situation is overwhelming, and you'd rather not think about it for a while longer. But you're driving me crazy!" Zane drove his hips forward again. "Either spank me or fuck me, please!"

Grinning, Cole continued his teasing caress, sliding his palm over the firm cheeks of the man's bum and down his thighs. He nudged them apart and slipped a hand between those sturdy columns of muscle and bone, cupping the warm, round sac. "Spank you? Have you misbehaved? Do you need a spanking?" Cole was intrigued. He'd never spanked anyone before.

"For fuck's sake, just do me, would you?" Zane snarled, his temper obviously getting the better of him.

Cole loved trying new things and wasn't about to let Zane off so easily. He pressed his free arm across the man's back, holding him in place, while continuing to toy with the hefty ball sac and the crack of his arse.

Zane's writhing grew more desperate when Cole pushed a finger against the tight rosebud nestled between his cheeks. He groaned when it popped inside.

"So, fucking or spanking?" Cole twisted his digit around the tight passage. His own cock shifted, pulsing under the weight of his new lover.

"Whatever you want. Fuck, spank, I don't care," Zane growled. "Just don't leave me hanging."

"And you said *I* was always horny. What about you and this monster you have dangling between your legs?" Popping his finger free, Cole pushed his hand between them and grabbed Zane's impressive hard-on.

"Yes," the man hissed and pumped his hips.

"Yes, you want to fuck, or yes, you want a spanking?" Cole asked, insistent. "Make a choice or you get neither."

"Fuck then, fuck me," Zane replied quickly. He raised his arse, perhaps hoping Cole would relent and slip a finger back into his tight hole.

"I think I want to spank you, first." Cole released the hard shaft and laid his palm on the nearest cheek. He waited until he sensed the time was right, then raised his hand, preparing for the first blow.

Peering over his shoulder, Zane must have seen what he was doing, because suddenly, his bum cheeks clenched tight. "Then spank me," he said with a hint of mischief in his voice.

"Turn around, don't look." Cole expected an argument but got none. The beautiful, white-haired man simply turned his face away and put both his hands on the ground. Cole lowered his arm, again stroking the taut, tanned bottom, exploring the crease and the inside of the muscular thighs. The firm, round balls shifted, the sac grew tight and wrinkled under his touch. "I've never spanked anyone before, but it excites me to think about it."

"Just do something." Zane's voice was hoarse. He lifted his arse again.

"Spread your feet apart." Cole pushed against the smooth, inner thighs trapping his hand. A moment later, he had room to explore and tease, but instead he pulled away. The view was spectacular — two lush mounds of skin, divided by the dark cleft between and the soft pucker of a tight anus.

"Cole, you're driving me crazy." Zane shifted, pushing his cock forward.

"Yeah, I know. Fun, isn't it?"

There was a long pause, and several more shiftings of the man's feet, before he replied in a soft voice, "Yes, you bugger."

Chuckling, yet feeling hornier than he had in weeks, Cole brought his hand down with as much force as he could from such a short distance. The cheek he struck wobbled deliciously, and the howl that came from Zane was music to his ears. The blow turned into a caress, his hand moving around the buttock, examining the sudden heat.

It wasn't enough. Cole wanted more and raised his hand again. He waited for Zane to relax then spanked him on the other side.

"Youch!" Zane twisted and tried to roll onto the ground, but Cole held him.

Their cocks dragged across each other, both hard and both dripping pre-cum. Cole shuddered and ran his hand over the reddened flesh, admiring the blossoming handprints adorning each.

"You really do have an amazing arse, you know. It reddens nicely." He ran his hand over the upturned cheeks and again between them. Zane's sudden shiver told him he was doing the right thing, circling and tormenting the tight, crinkled hole. He pushed in, past the outer ring of muscle. "I love the feel of your hole gripping me." He gently eased it in and out, pushing it a little deeper with each inward thrust. When his palm rested flat over Zane's arse, he stopped and wiggled his inserted digit, probing for the hard nut of his prostate.

"Ay!" cried Zane. He pushed back into Cole's hand. "Your cock would feel good in there, too, you know. Much better than just your finger."

"Maybe." Cole pretended to ponder, while continuing to massage the small organ. Zane's cock throbbed every time Cole jammed his fingers against the man's prostate, and Cole was sure a climax wasn't far behind. "But if I moved you around so I could fuck you, I wouldn't get to watch this quite so easily."

"But you'd feel it, and I know I can make it good for you."

"I know that, too. We've fucked already, remember?"

"Yes," Zane hissed. Sweat glistened along his flesh, filling the hollow of his spine. "How could I forget? You're amazing when we fuck."

"Ah, and I adore when you talk dirty." Cole withdrew his single digit and worked two into the gripping hole. "Tell me how much you liked it. Tell me what you want me to do, now."

"I loved the feeling of your big cock piercing my hole. The softness of the crown popping inside was amazing. When you pushed the shaft in, I thought I'd lose consciousness. It just felt so good."

Cole spread his fingers, stretching the membrane, preparing the man for another such treat. "What about the spanking? Did you like me spanking you, first?"

"Yes, yes, I like the heat on my arse."

"You've done this before?"

"Damn, Cole. Fuck me. Please." Zane's hips trembled, the muscles in his arse clutching at Cole's fingers.

"Horny bugger, aren't you?" Cole pushed a third finger into the hungry hole and worked all three in and out.

"Fuck yeah, you know I am."

"Tell me how you want it." He was enjoying the dialogue too much to let it stop. His cock felt like it was on fire. Each gentle thrusting of his fingers brought an unmistakable squirming of his lover's hips, which dragged their cocks against each other in a wonderfully erotic way. Pre-cum anointed them both and made the stimulation that much better. The smell of arousal hung heavy in the air.

"Let me lean over that log, the one right next to us. I'll spread my legs good and wide. You'll have no trouble getting into me."

"What if I want something else?" He smiled, knowing he was frustrating the poor man nearly beyond endurance.

"What? Tell me what you want." Zane twisted his upper body around so he could look up at Cole. "Whatever you like. I'll do it." His eyes were wide, his nostrils flared and his face and shoulders were flushed bright red.

Pulling his fingers from the warm dampness of the hole, Cole said, "Go drape yourself over the log."

He watched appreciatively as the tall, well-built man tumbled off his lap. With his handsome, pre-cum-lubricated cock flailing between his legs, he rushed to arrange himself over the fallen tree. Cole sat and admired the view for a few seconds before climbing to his feet and following. When he was less than a body length from the luscious arse, he dropped to his knees and approached him at a slow crawl. The smell of the man dragged a moan from deep inside Cole. Finally, near enough, he leaned forward, flicking his tongue along the backside of Zane's thigh, and smiled at the shuddering reaction.

"Keep still," he commanded.

"I'll try. You're making me crazy."

Cole leaned in again and slid his tongue from the back of Zane's knee to the crease joining leg to bum. He ran the tip along the delicate tuck of skin and then into the warm groove. Targeting the man's hole, he lapped at the tight swirl of tissue, pushing his tongue barely within. Zane's pungent taste forced a groan of pleasure from deep inside Cole.

"Oh fuck, oh fuck!"

Zane's soft litany was music to Cole, urging him to delve even deeper into the man's anus.

He reached up and cupped the dangling ball sac. He tugged gently on the precious orbs until he heard a deep intake of breath. Pulling away, he whispered huskily, "Yeah, I like you crazy. Don't move."

"Right. Not moving." Zane shuffled his feet, perhaps trying to position himself more comfortably, more likely attempting to wedge his toes under the log.

Cole trailed a line of kisses from one taut, muscular buttock to the other, bypassing his lover's anus. He gathered saliva in his mouth and, on the return trip, spat it onto the waiting hole.

Rising to his feet, Cole gave his cock several caressing strokes. He was hot and wanted nothing more than to drive his aching shaft deep into the man's arse. He knew he couldn't, the pain would be unbearable. He stepped forward, crouched and took his cock firmly in hand.

Positioning himself just so, he nudged the sensitive head against the pucker. He shuddered, the sensation causing him to doubt his ability to control the animal lust rising inside him.

"Do it." Zane pushed his arse back, attempting to trap Cole's weeping cock head. "Fuck me, I'm ready. More than ready."

"I said, hold still." Cole strained for control. Without warning, he raised his free hand and brought it down twice, once per cheek, as hard as he could. To his credit, Zane kept still, but the yelp of surprise made Cole smile even wider. While the man beneath him was still gasping from the swats, Cole wedged his cock head at the opening again and pushed.

He slipped in easily, the sudden heat and grip of the man's arse a sensation he'd never tire of. He eased forward, stopping only when his shaft was half-buried. Breathing deeply, he released the hold he had on his cock and moved both hands to Zane's hips. Gripping firmly, he swayed Zane's body from side to side, enjoying the way his cock head pressed against the different parts of Cole's arse. Slowly he sank in deeper, feeling the stretch of anal membrane around his shaft, the heat enveloping more of him the further he went. Blissful release was close. His balls churned with the desire to spend, and soon. He fought it off, wanting desperately to pleasure his new lover, first.

"Don't tease me any more. Fuck me. I need it." Zane pressed back against him. Arse met groin with a resounding slap of flesh.

Tightening his grip, Cole held him firmly in place until he was sure he could go on without shooting too soon. He began the slow, easy dance of fuck, driving in and out, each thrust a little faster, a little firmer. Every few strokes, he ground his pelvis into Zane's behind and growled his pleasure. When his heart raced, he let go of his control and slammed into his lover's tight buttocks.

"Yes, yes," Zane hissed repeatedly, encouraging him to greater speed.

Cole reached around the man's belly and took hold of his lover's cock. The stiff shaft filled his hand. He pumped it, and pre-cum coated his fingers in only a few strokes. It pulsed and thickened, and he knew the inevitable climax was mere moments away.

His own came like a blast of fireworks, exploding into the tight confines of his partner's arse as his body tensed, and his hips shot forward. He lost sight and hearing. All that mattered was the driving of his hips, the squeezing of his shaft, and Zane's sticky cum shooting in stream after stream through his fingers.

He throbbed and gasped until there was nothing left then he collapsed over Zane's back. Sweat-slicked and hot, it was like lying on a bed of smooth, warm stone.

"Thank you," Zane sighed. "But you better get off me, or I'm going to fall over."

Chuckling, Cole replied, "I was just wondering how I was going to manage that without collapsing, myself."

Pulling back, he eased himself out of the tight hole then dropped to the grass in a trembling heap. Zane joined him, arms and legs winding around his.

"That was amazing." The white-tressed man turned his face upwards and pressed his lips to Cole's.

When he broke the kiss a few moments later, Cole looked into the man's brilliant blue eyes. He wanted to sink into them and lose himself. "Yes, that was truly amazing. We're good together." He stopped there, unwilling to offer more than the occasional, afternoon fuck session. There were so many others he hadn't tried, so many men and women he wanted to test and explore. But those eyes, those lips, affected him like no one else's had. The man made him feel as if he could do anything.

"The talisman, what are you going to do about that?" Zane asked as he sat up. His face showed his concern.

Cole knew the pack couldn't be without a leader for long. Not now. Not after the fire. The entire tribe needed strong guidance. Yet, he wasn't ready to settle down, let alone take on that kind of responsibility. Hell, he didn't have a life-mate, so the talisman couldn't belong to him.

"I don't know. It can only belong to someone who has the good of the pack in his heart, and a life-mate who will also do all he or she can for the tribe. That's not me. I'm too young." He pushed himself away from the beautiful, white-haired man and got to his feet. He went to where his clothing lay in a pile. Bending over, he retrieved the brilliant red-stoned talisman. Looking at it, he mused, "It's beautiful. But not for me. I'm not ready, not yet."

"Maybe the amulet knows something you don't." Zane retrieved his own pile of clothing shed earlier and began to dress.

Cole watched him, eyes fixed on the man's arse. Zane hopped on one long, well-muscled leg and stuffed his foot into the leather pants. A moment later, he pushed the other one in and then his bum was covered, concealed from view. Still Cole watched him, admiring the lean body, the beautifully shaped shoulders and arms. He loved how the man's silky, white hair swung across his lower back. He found himself wondering if he could coax Zane into another session.

"Are you going to stare at me all afternoon?"

Cole looked up and smiled into his lover's face. "I was just wondering if I could convince you to take those clothes off again. You make me horny."

"Horny?" Zane gaped. "But...but you just came. You're insatiable."

Winking, Cole replied, "Yeah, I know, and you love me for it."

Cocking his head, the amazing man said, "Maybe that's part of the reason."

Shrugging Zane's remark off, Cole returned his attention to the amulet. "We should get back to the pack. They'll wonder where we are. We've got to tell them about Gar and his lover. Damn!"

Zane approached him and, after laying both hands on his shoulders, said, "Yes, we do. And then we have to explain how the talisman has chosen you."

"But it can't. I'm not fit to be the next guardian. I've got too many wild oats to sow yet and I have no mate. It can't be me."

"Then let me hold it." Zane lowered one hand and held it open.

Cole looked at the outstretched palm. He glanced down at the delicate, gold filigree and the red stone at its centre then tucked it in close to his chest, protectively. "Maybe later," he whispered. *Maybe not.*

* * * *

They were still a good half-day's journey away from their pack. The trip might have gone more quickly had they shifted into wolves, but Cole wanted to gather things along the way the pack could use, and that was easier when he was in human form.

They'd stopped to help a small bear clan bury one of their dead. After wrapping the body, they'd watched the clan members lift it into a tree so the old man could begin his journey to join the Great Spirit. The bears had ancient customs, very much like their own.

We have to do the same. The pack must pull itself together and take care of our dead. With their leader gone, it might fall apart. He thought guiltily about the bodies of Gar and Ruby that he'd discovered and left behind. Charred and burned as they were, he truly thought their spirits had already gone wherever they were going. There was nothing he or Zane could have done for them. But he knew something was needed to mark the passing of such important members of the tribe.

Trudging forward, he glanced sideways at his travelling companion. Zane had only been with the pack a few months. Details about his prior life and pack were sketchy. Cole gathered something about an unfortunate run-in with hunters from the nearby city of Newburgen. Zane had done what he could to help his brothers, but the others had succumbed to their injuries. He alone had survived. He didn't like to talk about it, so Cole hadn't pressed.

The white-haired warrior had apparently told Gar everything, and their leader had welcomed him into his family pack without hesitation. Cole had been curious at the time, but more interested in the man himself. Tall, with muscles bulging in all the right places, he was the most gorgeous creature Cole had ever laid eyes on. If his own sexual orientation had been in doubt before, it wasn't any longer with the arrival of handsome, sexy Zane. He definitely liked men as much as, or possibly even more than, he did women.

Gar had been tribal leader long before Cole was a pup. He was probably Cole's uncle or some more distant relative related by blood, but he'd never been the mentor type. Growing up, Cole had learned much more from Kaleb and Ulric, two mated males in his pack. Their relationship was a source of awe and inspiration for him. Inherently sexual, playful and loyal, while also enjoying the occasional inclusion into their bed of a female they both admired and agreed upon, those wolves had what Cole wanted. *Someday.*

His closeness with Kaleb had irritated Gar, who'd had plans to mate Cole with his female offspring, Tala. No matter how pretty the raven-haired she-wolf was, though, she did nothing for Cole. He knew he was nowhere near settling down, but when he did, it wouldn't be with her.

He kicked a rock as he marched forward.

"You're quiet." Zane fell into step with him.

"Ever fucked a female?" Cole found the same rock on the path and kicked it again.

Zane coughed. "Where the devil did that come from?"

"Just thinking."

"Well then, sure I have. It's actually quite pleasurable. They're deliciously soft and tender. I simply prefer the smell and ruggedness of a male." He glanced at Cole. "How about you? You ever been with a female?"

"Yeah, of course." He had, but all the encounters had been as a wolf, and there'd been nothing tender about any of them. Pure, animal fucking was an appropriate description — quick and satisfying, a means to an end for both himself and his female partners.

Before Zane came along, none of his sexual encounters had held much meaning. They felt damn good, though, so he arranged fuck sessions as often as he could. He'd told himself that was all he needed. The females had all been satisfied, he was sure of that.

Yet watching Kaleb and Ulric interact, whether as wolves or men, fascinated him. The caring tenderness they showed each other never failed to amaze and arouse him. Their mating was truly lovemaking, whether they were in a secluded spot in the forest or sprawled atop the pile of thick furs in their den.

Cole suspected they knew he observed them at every opportunity. Kaleb always stuck up for him and had gone several go-rounds with Gar about the younger man and his sexuality. Allowing him to watch seemed to be Kaleb's way of teaching Cole — gently guiding him in the ways of love.

"Have a specific female in mind?" Zane's comment broke the silence.

"No! Fuck no!" Cole leaned towards him and pressed their mouths together. His tongue traced the seam of Zane's lips, and he groaned when they parted, allowing him access.

Everything Cole had been carrying fell to the ground as he grasped Zane and pulled his body close.

"Damn," Zane managed to mutter. He dropped his armload of scavenged items and deepened the kiss then pulled back regretfully. "We'll never make it back at this rate, but who cares? I can be out of these pants in a flash if you'd like to give me a better idea of what you're thinking about."

The offer was tempting. It wouldn't take long to bend the tall man over and ream his arse again, thoroughly and completely. The very idea made Cole's cock twitch. But they had a job to do, and they'd dawdled enough that day. Their pack needed them. They had to get back.

Another thought niggled at Cole. He craved more than a quick, mindless fuck. Waiting until they were home and could take their time, enjoy each other languorously, sounded very nice. He knew Zane would like it better, and for some reason, that seemed important. He kissed Zane once more. "Much as I'd enjoy that, we should get going. We need to travel with the daylight. But don't tire yourself out too much. When we get back, you're all mine."

Zane scooped up the items he'd been carrying and scooted ahead on the path, glancing back teasingly. "Maybe. We'll see."

Grabbing the various bits of metal, cloth and leather he'd thought might be useful back at the den, Cole did a double step to catch up, grinning. "Sounds like someone's asking for trouble."

"Me, trouble?" Zane peered over his shoulder and blinked innocently. "If you feel that way, you might have to spank me again."

"Fuck." Cole shook his head to clear the lustful images. He was hard in an instant just thinking about it.

Obviously, he and Zane had barely begun to explore the possibilities in their relationship.

The path ended, and they were forced to wade through knee-deep, blackened grass. Cole frowned. It was hard to get excited about the future when the present was so damned dim.

"The going would be easier if we shifted." Zane swiped at a tall weed using his free arm like a machete.

"I, uh, wouldn't be able to carry this stuff." Cole held up the scraps in his hands.

"That would be a vital loss to the pack." Zane's eyebrows waggled as he smiled at Cole.

Uncomfortable with hiding his true reason, Cole smiled half-heartedly. If they morphed into wolves they could only carry packs, or whatever could go around their necks. They had no knapsacks with them, and he wasn't prepared to place the talisman around his neck—yet. A worry nagged at the back of his mind. *Once the amulet goes on, how can I be sure it'll come off?* With another quick glance at his lover, he walked on.

* * * *

They stopped for a meal of jerky and berries a short distance from home. Zane dipped his face into the nearby stream and gulped water.

Watching the tall man stretch and move, Cole had to tamp down the stirrings of his ever-ready cock. They were almost at their den. Once they'd talked to the rest of the pack and filled them in with news of their grisly discovery, the rest of the evening would be theirs, or so he hoped.

"Water's nice and cool. Join me for a drink—or a dip?" Zane's eyes seared into Cole's, the lust mirroring his own.

"We're almost home. The pack is waiting for us."

"All the more reason to fuck me now. They're going to be upset and full of questions. We'll be up half the night explaining, comforting."

Cole scowled. "I don't see why. They're not our responsibility." Even as he said it, he knew it wasn't true. He hated to admit it, though.

"Of course they are. They're our family." Zane sauntered over and stood in front of him. "Have you forgotten the amulet you carry in your pocket? If nothing else, that makes them our responsibility."

"My, aren't you the conscientious one?" Cole cupped Zane's groin. "Maybe I do need to turn you over my knee and paddle you for being such a know-it-all."

"Never said I knew it all. I do know the difference between right and wrong." He thrust his hips forward and gazed into Cole's eyes. "And I know I'd like more of that. Spank me first, if you like, but then I expect to be fucked properly."

"Cheeky bastard." Cole squeezed the hardening shaft in his hand. Zane was right. The pack would need more from him than dropping the bombshell and running. He shook his head to clear the stupidity. This responsibility thing would either make him stronger or fucking kill him.

A rustle in the brush next to them caught Cole's attention. He glanced over and examined the scraggly bushes. "Did you hear something?"

Zane's gaze followed his. "Probably a rabbit. Quit trying to change the subject. I swear, you like teasing me, more than anyone I've ever known. I'll put up with your agonising taunts for just so long, then they may backfire on you. You might find your arse over a log with me taking matters into my own hands."

"That a threat?" Cole grinned and made eye contact. The idea of being taken by the strong man was hot. He could get into some of that action.

Another movement in the bushes made Cole freeze. He kept his face straight ahead and peered out of the corner of his eyes, speaking quietly. "That was no rabbit."

"No, it wasn't." Zane spoke just as low, while turning slowly to face the brush. "Neither is that."

A dark-headed child stood watching them, her long, brown hair dishevelled and her eyes full of fear.

"What the fuck?" Cole muttered then gaped as the child turned and sprinted off.

Chapter Two

Cole loped after the child and heard Zane at his heel. Their small quarry had an advantage, being lower to the ground. Most of the foliage had burned off the bushes, leaving gaps below but prickly shards higher up, at the perfect level to scratch their arms and faces.

"Ouch!" Zane muttered when the branch Cole let loose swatted him.

"Shit. Sorry." He paused. "Did you see which way she went?"

"No, all I saw was a thorny limb flying at me." Zane rubbed his cheek.

"She was just here." Cole glanced around and spotted the little one, frozen against a tree trunk. "There!" He dropped what he'd been carrying and dove towards the child, but someone sprang between them, blocking his path.

"Leave her alone!" The voice was female, but the tone was all mother wolf.

Cole stumbled to a halt. Zane stopped short next to him and would have fallen if he hadn't grabbed Cole's arm for support.

Awestruck, Cole looked at the growling figure, her arms poised to defend herself and the youngster she protected. She was nowhere near his height, but the mass of long, unruly red hair made her appear so. Her face was dirty and her clothes, if they could be called that, mere rags that clung to her abundant curves.

Cole held up his hands in a gesture of surrender. "I wasn't trying to harm the child. She startled us, and we only wanted to find out who she is and what she's doing out here alone. We're trying to help."

When the child disappeared into the brush, she lowered her hands slightly and studied the men. Cole thought she almost sniffed at them.

"Who are you?" she asked. "Townspeople from Newburgen? It's unwise to come so far into the woods without weapons. Never know who you might run into." A low rumble sounded in the back of her throat.

Cole glanced at Zane, and they smiled at each other. He looked back at the female, admiring her attempt at bravado. "We're not from Newburgen. We're members of a pack that lives nearby. And as for weapons, we can acquire them quickly enough, if needed."

She stared at them questioningly.

Zane spoke quietly. "What do you think, Cole? Is she wolfen?"

Cole kept his eyes on her. "It would appear so."

The female took a deep, shuddering breath, a look of surprise on her filthy face.

Very slowly, Cole pulled the crystal-clear red amulet from his pocket. He held it up. The gold filigree forming the wolf's head shone brilliantly.

She gasped. "The talisman. Then you're—"

"Members of the wolf tribe. We're returning to our den after scouting out damage from the fire. The forest has taken quite a hit."

"You're not the tribe leader. I've never seen him, but I heard he was old and wise." She tugged self-consciously at the scraps of fabric, which barely covered her ample breasts and hips.

"Yes. He was." Cole nodded. "Gar was our tribal and pack leader. He and his mate, Ruby, died in the fire. The amulet has not yet chosen a new holder."

She stared at the dangling talisman, which to Cole's amazement glowed ever so faintly.

Zane smiled. "Personally, I believe it has."

Cole gave him a grim look and turned back to the female. "No, it hasn't."

She raised her eyebrows. "I'd tend to agree with your friend." Setting her shoulders proudly, she continued, "I'm Shira, also of the wolf tribe. The fire decimated my pack. We've been out here for days, trying to decide what to do and where to go."

"At least you're not alone." Cole gazed at her evenly.

Her eyes narrowed, then she seemed to give in. He couldn't tell if she trusted them, but she seemed tired of carrying the burden by herself. "No, I'm not alone. Another female of my pack escaped with me. And we have two pups."

Cole smiled. "The little dark-eyed creature we were chasing. She's fast."

Shira nodded. "We've had to be. It's been frightening, on our own. We've had nothing but water and a few roots —" She bit back whatever else she was going to say. A pink flush raced across her chest and face. "She's shy."

So proud! The two females had survived the inferno, managing to rescue their two pups, yet this one seemed hesitant to appear needy. Cole liked her spirit already. He reached into his pocket and felt around. Removing a cloth, he gently uncovered several pieces of jerky. "I wonder if she could be coaxed out with a little something to eat? It's not much, but we're only a short distance from our den. It might hold you until then."

"I've got more." Zane held out another pouch. "In case anyone else would like some."

Shira studied the dried meat intently. "The pups could use a meal."

"There's a clearing with several tree stumps just over there." Cole motioned to the side. "Why don't you call them to join us?"

Two scruffy children and an equally unkempt female appeared from out of the brush, eyeing them nervously.

"Good." Cole smiled warmly at them. "Let's go sit for a spell and have a bite to eat." He turned towards the clearing and shoved the amulet back in his pocket.

Zane followed, the others close behind.

Cole sat on a stump and held out the jerky. "My name is Cole. This is Zane. We live in a den not far from here."

The two females sat a little distance from him. Hesitantly, they both reached for the jerky and passed some to the pups. They all chewed vigorously as they kept their focus on the men. "This is Meghan." Shira nodded towards her yellow-haired companion. She glanced at the pups as she ate. "Skip and Hani."

"Hello, Skip. Hello, Hani." Cole acknowledged each of the youngsters who watched him cautiously. "Meghan."

The female didn't speak, just nodded and ate as quickly as she could. They were obviously half-starved and in shock.

"This has been a trying time for you." Zane watched them, kind concern on his face. "The fire was frightening for us all. You've lost so much."

The female pup sat, wide-eyed and chewing determinedly for a few moments, before she spoke hesitantly. "It was all around us, the fire. It was horrible. People were yelling and running all over. Shira got burned getting us out of our den."

"Hani." Shira looked at her sternly.

The child closed her mouth and went back to chewing her piece of dried meat.

"Are you injured?" Cole asked quickly. The foursome was so dirty, it was hard to tell. With the river so close, they'd surely had the opportunity to bathe since the blaze had died out. Unless they were badly burned. *Or scared beyond belief.*

"Minor wounds." She brushed him off.

Something about the female captivated him. She was beautiful—shapely in all the right places, with full breasts and curvy hips—but it was more than that. Her feisty demeanour, even in the face of catastrophe, was engaging. "As I mentioned, our den is a short distance from here. We have medical supplies, clean clothing..." he watched Shira devour the last of her jerky and lick her fingers, "and food. Plenty for all."

"We're fine." Meghan's voice echoed Shira's defiance.

"The rest of your pack?" Zane asked gently.

"Everyone is gone," Skip murmured in a quiet, distant voice, as if he couldn't quite believe it.

Cole exchanged glances with Zane. *Then they're not exactly fine.* Two females with two young pups were easy pickings in the wild, no matter how spunky they were. Cole chose his words carefully. The last thing he wanted to do was offend. "Obviously, you are fine. The fact you rescued your pups and managed to save yourselves is a great testament to your fortitude. Perhaps you could use some safe shelter for the night. Take a meal, clean up, rest. We extend our pack's hospitality to you."

The females gazed at each other nervously, and Shira asked, "The others in your pack would not object?"

Zane sighed. "We're saddled with the great misfortune of returning to our pack with the bad news about Gar and Ruby."

"Bitter medicine to swallow, indeed." Shira gazed at them thoughtfully. "Perhaps we shouldn't intrude."

"I think the distraction would do everyone a world of good." Cole smiled at her over the heads of the pups. "Our females love to mother cute, little pups. Yive and Tala will be all over these two."

"We're their family!" Meghan exclaimed, anxiety registering in her eyes.

"Of course, you are. No one will try to take them from you." Zane held up his hands. "Yive has two thriving pups of her own. Cole simply meant that you're welcome in our pack, and that you and the pups would fit right in. Whatever we have to offer, we do so willingly."

Shira gazed from Cole to Zane before bowing her head. "We accept your kindness."

"No!" Meghan drew her aside, and they whispered harshly to one another. Cole observed the pups sitting in silence, consuming the rest of their meal, until the she-wolves returned to the circle of stumps.

"We'll consent to your thoughtfulness—for the night." Shira nodded. "Thank you."

Cole smiled. In the small clan of Meghan, Shira and the two pups, the red-haired she-wolf was obviously dominant. *I wouldn't want to cross her.* Thoughts of other things he *would* want to do to her and with her floated through his mind, but Cole tamped them down, quickly glancing away.

Damnation! Just when he'd about decided that Zane was the one he wanted to explore fully, and intended to do so at every opportunity, a new wrinkle appeared in the fabric. His eyes darted to Shira's round breasts, and he found himself wondering how the soft weight of them would feel in the palms of his hands. Cole shook his head to clear it.

The sun was fading quickly. Despite their bravado, his newfound charges were depending on him and Zane to see them to the safety of the pack's den. For the second time that day, the tug of responsibility niggled at him. It was an unfamiliar emotion, and one with which he wasn't quite sure how to deal.

Cole patted his thighs and stood. "We'd best get moving or we'll lose the light. With the pack in such turmoil, I'd rather approach when they can see us." He gathered the items he'd scavenged.

Zane got to his feet, and the two women trudged beside them. The cubs bounded from their perches on the log. Filthy they might be, but the two youngsters seemed in fine shape. The women had done well by them.

He watched the small group closely and, after only a moment or so, realised Shira favoured her left side. She was injured, burned most likely, but too proud to ask for help. He'd keep an eye on her. Stubborn was one thing, but he wouldn't allow her to go unattended if she needed meds.

"Zane, would you bring up the rear?" he asked and pointed his chin towards Shira. "Make sure the pups don't wander, if you can."

As if he could read Cole's mind, Zane eyed the redheaded female and gave a sharp nod. "You bet. Just don't go too fast. These two look as if they're about done in."

"We're fine," Shira said in a tight voice.

"Yes, you're fine, but you're exhausted. Anyone would be after what you've been through." Cole stood in front of her, refusing to back down.

Her lips started out tight, a pale line of determination, but they softened as he watched. Her chin quivered, and, for a moment, he was afraid she was going to break. He quickly said, "We'll get you all to the den then we'll worry about what comes next."

She looked up at him, her eyes sparkling with unshed tears. "Thank you," she whispered then lowered her gaze.

Cole turned and checked his surroundings. It definitely wouldn't do for them to get lost. The terrain appeared so different with the forest burnt in so many areas. It took a moment, but he spotted the familiar range of hills and headed just slightly to the left.

He kept his pace a little slower than he was used to, hoping to give the females an easy time on this leg of the journey. Behind him, he heard a soft moan every so often and wondered how badly Shira was burned.

The charred area gave way to greener patches of brush and trees, only to revert to blackened swaths of dead vegetation. Cole clambered over fallen logs and turned to help the women cross. The pups scampered ahead, but Zane called them back after they'd gone a few dozen paces.

"But we want to see what's up there," Skip, the more adventurous of the pair, whined as he trudged back to the group.

Cole paused to watch the youngsters return to their places in the line.

"You'll see soon enough," Meghan admonished from behind Shira. She, too, was showing signs of distress, staggering over the blackened branches strewn across their path.

"Very soon," Cole said, and wondered at how protective he suddenly felt for the four waifs.

Shira glanced up at him but quickly looked away when he gazed down at her. *Such a gorgeous creature,* he thought, and looked over her to where Zane stood at the end of the line.

The tall, white-haired man winked at him and smiled.

Cole turned and resumed their trek. His thoughts raced, going from the known excitement of his lust for Zane to the unknown cravings he harboured for Shira. They had him confused and exasperated. Her figure, scarcely concealed by her ragged, filthy clothing, seemed branded into his mind. Her breasts, with their plump, tanned flesh, nuzzled against each other every time she moved. The smooth curve of her waist into her hip seemed made for his hand, and he longed to place one there. Her legs were long enough to bring her up to his collarbone if she stood very tall. Her brilliant, blue eyes captivated him whenever their gazes met.

He stumbled over a root, and a rush of sudden heat warmed his face. "Damn," he cursed softly, dragging his attention back to their trek home. The crotch of his pants was too tight, and he reached down to re-arrange himself. His erection pressed against his hand, and he gave it a surreptitious squeeze.

Am I lusting after Shira or Zane?

The small group emerged from a dense swath of forest onto a wide patch of relatively green grass. A creek meandered from somewhere in the foothills, and across it was the slope of the mountains and the pack's winter den where they'd sought refuge. The half dozen pale grey mounds of ash in front of it stood as a testament to the fire's damage.

"There's home." Cole wasn't sure how he felt about arriving, but it was too late to turn back. One of the pack pups had spotted them and whooped their arrival.

"There goes our chance at a quiet entrance," Zane said.

Cole's stomach twisted. He knew he'd have to break the news about Gar and his mate in a very short time. The talisman grew warm, heating his thigh through the pocket of his pants.

A few minutes later, the pack was all around them, welcoming them home, examining their finds and reaching out to touch the newcomers. Dib and Effie, the two pups belonging to the pack, found Skip and Hani. After an initial uneasiness, accompanied by much sniffing and posturing, the four pups scampered off, yipping and pouncing on each other in some type of chasing game. Shira and Meghan huddled together while the pack questioned Cole and Zane about what they had seen and done.

Cole tried to hang back, but Tala, Gar's chunky, dark-haired daughter, confronted him. "What did you find? Did you see any sign of my father or Ruby?" Crossing her plump arms, she glared up at him.

From the other side of the crowd, Zane replied, "Tala, we have guests who need attention."

The female turned and glared at Zane. "I want to know if you found my father. Is that such a difficult question?"

On one of the outside tables, Cole deposited the odds and ends he'd collected then placed a hand on her shoulder. Those around him fell back, as if giving him room to break the news. His heart went out to her. She wasn't his type, but she was a pack member and, for some strange reason, it seemed important that he tell her gently. "Let me get our guests settled, then we'll all talk. Will you help me, Tala?"

She looked up into his eyes, her own softening under the impact of his. "Yes, of course I will. What happened to them?"

"They've lost everything to the fire. Their pack was destroyed. There's just the four of them left."

"Oh my god." Her hand went to her face, and she glanced at the two women still clinging to each other off to one side. "I'm so sorry. Are they hurt? They must be starving. Have they been on their own all this time?"

"Shira, the red-head, she's been burned. Won't tell me how bad, though. She's been favouring her left side."

She turned from him and went towards Shira and Meghan, her arms outstretched in welcome. "You poor dears, you must be exhausted," she said when she got closer.

Shira moved away and pulled Meghan with her. Straightening up, she pushed her shoulders back and, in a strong voice, replied, "We're fine. We just need a little rest and some food for the pups."

Cole looked at her and felt a rush of pride and caring that surprised him. She was so strong, so vibrant, yet he knew she was half-starved and in a great deal of pain.

Tala lowered her hands. "Please, won't you let us help you? We've all lost so much to the fire."

Shira sagged a little then, her shoulders drooped and her stern-faced demeanour softened. She looked first at Cole then back to Tala and replied, "Thank you. Yes. We've lost much."

"Come with me, you'll want to bathe and then eat, both of you." She ushered the two women away, taking them towards the mouth of the den.

Cole was sure they'd be tended to. Tala had a great motherly instinct.

He was about to join Zane when Kaleb came through the group towards him. His mentor, who was barely ten years older than he was, looked old and tired, the pressure of the last week had obviously taken a toll. Tall and well built, the man's dark hair hung to the middle of his back in a rat's nest of soot and dirt from whatever cleanup work he'd undertaken.

Kaleb took him by the shoulders and hugged him close. "Welcome home, Cole. How is it out there?"

Extricating himself from the hug, Cole replied, "Not good. Can we go into the den? We've been walking for hours." Any hope he'd had of getting away with Zane for a little quiet time seemed farfetched then. But he knew they'd never leave him alone until he told the news.

"Surely. Why don't you go inside and take a load off, while I go clean up a little? I've been scavenging in the burned-out huts, trying to find anything that's still of use."

"Did you find much?" Zane's voice came from behind him, and Cole turned to give his new lover a quick smile.

"Not really. The fire destroyed whatever it touched. Some dried meat we'd taken from here when we left in the spring and a few hides. That's about it. It's a good thing the caves here held a lot of supplies."

"We're better off than some." Cole reminded them of the four newcomers.

"True." Kaleb turned and headed for the stream. "I'll be back in a few. Go get something to eat. You must be famished. We'll talk when I return."

"Thanks, Kaleb." Cole grabbed Zane's arm and dragged him along as he headed for the den's entrance. The others followed, some talking softly while others seemed content to simply head for the security of the cave.

The few trees they passed were still standing, but had been scorched at the base. The grass was gone, the shrubs, little more than skeletal sticks pointing at the sky. Even the rocks and boulders littering the area were blackened or cracked from the heat of the fire.

Leaning against him, Zane whispered, "I want you."

Cole looked at the handsome man and smiled. "You have such a way with words."

"Yeah, I know. It's a talent."

"You've got other talents. One or two that absolutely drive me wild."

Zane's smile widened, and he slid a hand down over Cole's arse. Cupping it, he whispered, "I know, and I want to drive you wild again."

Sighing, Cole replied, "That's going to have to wait. I was crazy when I thought I could just tell them about Gar and Ruby then leave. I have a feeling it's going to take a while."

The amulet grew warm against his thigh. It was almost as if the blood red stone was sending him some kind of message. He pushed his hand into his pocket and wrapped his fingers around the talisman. The heat pulsed and sent comforting warmth up his arm.

He let the stone go and drew out his hand as they made their way into the den. Going from the early evening sunlight to the dimness of the cave, he slowed his pace for a moment until his eyes adjusted. The smell of the pack was rich when he inhaled deeply.

The others wandered into their separate dens, small alcoves that circled the central chamber, leaving him and

Zane to themselves. The fire pit in the middle of the room was unlit, but ready. By some unspoken signal, they went and stood by the rough wooden benches surrounding it.

Cole turned to face Zane and pulled him close. "I'm hoping this won't take all night, but I'm not counting on it. You can hang out in my den if you want. I'll come to you as soon as I can."

Zane pressed his lips to Cole's throat. Cole found the kiss comforting, yet it carried such a yearning heat, it took his breath.

When Zane pulled away, his voice was husky with passion. "I'll stay. I'd rather be with you here than waiting alone for you to come to me." He kissed Cole again then, with his lips still against his throat, he murmured, "At least I'll be able to see you. I want to be here for you, even if I do plan to tease you unmercifully later."

Chuckling, Cole said, "Oh, yeah? Just what do you think you're going to do?"

"Haven't decided yet, but I'm sure something will come to mind."

Cole reached around the man and clasped his arse. Squeezing the firm globes tight, he pulled Zane closer. "You'll get that spanking if you're not careful."

"Promises, promises."

A noise behind him dragged Cole's attention reluctantly away from his lover. The man was quickly becoming more than a quick fuck. Cole wanted something else, as well. He wanted to give him pleasure. He wanted to make him happy.

Giving his head a shake, he cleared the thoughts of lust away. Kaleb and his mate Ulric strode into the chamber from outside. Both males were large and well-muscled, though Kaleb was taller, and his dark hair hung to the middle of his back when he left it free, as it was now. Ulric, whose hair was lighter and hung in tight waves to his shoulders, had a small scar on his face that blazed red when he was angry.

"Have you gotten something to eat?" Kaleb asked, heading for the kitchen area at the rear of the cave.

Cole stepped away from Zane, but not too far. He felt incredibly protective suddenly. "No, not yet. We have news that we need to share with the pack. Food can wait."

Kaleb stopped and turned back to face him. "I see. Shall we get everyone out here?"

The others must have heard, because slowly they came out of their dens to lean against the rough stone walls. None came too close to Cole. Each of the family units, cousins for the most part, stayed together. It was as if they needed the reassurance. Zane was the only completely unrelated member.

Cole looked around, judging that all were present who needed to be. Even the two women, Shira and Meghan, peered from the kitchen alcove.

"We found Gar and Ruby," Cole said in a voice he was sure would carry to them all. He turned and looked at Zane, then back at Kaleb, his teacher and friend. "They're dead. The fire got them."

"No!" The anguished cry came from the kitchen.

Cole turned, just in time to see Tala launch herself at him. "No, it can't be. He can't be dead!" she screeched while flailing her fists against Cole's chest.

He grabbed her shoulders, holding her back until she stopped striking him. When her face softened and tears poured down her cheeks, he pulled her into his arms. Stroking her back, he whispered, "I'm so sorry, Tala, but he's gone. Ruby and your father are in a better place, now. They were together, and I'm sure that's how they would have wanted to go."

She sniffled into his chest for a few moments then murmured, "Where are their bodies?"

"About half a day's walk from here. It won't be possible to bring them back, I'm sorry. I thought a couple of us could return with shroud material and take care of them there." The thought formed in his mind at that moment and spilled out. It sounded much better than what he'd actually done, leaving the bodies where they were to be picked over by scavengers.

"Kaleb and I can do that." Ulric stepped forward. "We'll leave at first light tomorrow."

"I want to be there." Tala pushed away from Cole and wiped her eyes.

"I don't think that's wise. It wasn't an easy trip. I'm so sorry, Tala." Cole shook his head.

"It's my decision, not yours." She squinted up at him. "The talisman—did my father die wearing it? Did you find it?"

Uncomfortable, Cole shuffled his feet and looked at Tala. "Your father's body—I'm not sure you should—" He gazed to Kaleb for help.

"Cole's right, of course." Kaleb nodded, moving to Tala's side. "I agree with him about this. You don't want to remember your father this way. Let Ulric and me give him and Ruby the proper treatment. You know we'll show the utmost respect."

The look on Tala's face indicated she didn't want to go along with their decision, but perhaps felt she had no choice. "I'll leave it to you, Kaleb."

He squeezed her shoulders and planted a light kiss on her temple. "Have you seen to our guests, Tala? They appeared to be greatly in need of food and rest."

She glanced into the kitchen, where Shira and Meghan waited. "I'll do that now." Looking around for Yive, mother of the pack's two pups, she spotted her and said, "Would you gather the young ones? We'll feed them, too, and see about baths."

"Yes." Yive nodded and went to find the cubs.

Tala returned to the other women, and Cole saw them setting out trays of food on the table. His stomach rumbled.

Kaleb turned his back to the women. "You found the amulet, didn't you?"

Feeling guilty, Cole looked at him.

Kaleb smiled and nodded solemnly. "It glowed in your hands. I sense that."

"I don't want the blasted thing!" Cole muttered harshly. "I'm not ready for such responsibility, and even if I was, I don't have a mate! Everyone knows the talisman holder must be mated for life."

"Trust the wisdom of the talisman. If it chose you, then perhaps you're not as unsettled as you think."

Cole scowled. "Are you suggesting the talisman knows something I don't?"

"It usually does, my friend. I saw the looks your white-haired warrior sent your way. He's quite enamoured with you. I also saw how you looked at him."

"Uh, maybe." Unwilling to commit to anything, Cole answered vaguely. But in his heart, he felt an immense deal of pleasure, knowing Zane so obviously cared for him.

Kaleb chuckled. "On the other hand, I saw the way you watched over the wounded, red-headed she-wolf. She's quite a specimen, isn't she?"

"I, uh…" Cole was more confused than ever, and he groaned when the amulet again grew warm against his leg, right through his trousers. "I don't know what the fuck to do."

"Relax." Kaleb nudged his arm. "All will be revealed in time, I'm sure. Right now, you need food and rest. Go sit with the visitors and take your meal."

"Thank you, Kaleb." Cole exhaled when the older man walked away. His mentor seemed so wise, seemed to understand so many things Cole couldn't even begin to fathom. Attempting to figure it all out at the moment felt overwhelming. He turned and looked around, finally locating Zane. "Shall we grab a bite to eat?"

"Certainly." Zane smiled and allowed Cole to take the lead as they went to join the others.

"I hope you're being well-tended." Cole chose a seat at the table next to Shira, who was polishing off a serving of venison and berries.

"Your pack is very welcoming." She nodded. "Thank you."

He watched her wince as she squirmed in her seat. "Good. I do hope you'll allow Yive to treat your burns. Our healing powders will have you better in no time."

Her eyes clouded. "I might have to. We lost all our medicines to the fire."

Cole could see she was in great discomfort. He leaned in to reassure her and caught a whiff of she-wolf—her feminine scent tickled his nose with its heady, musky aroma. He paused, tamping down the feeling of his cock hardening. "Please do. You'll be...fine."

She gazed at him with a curious expression on her face. "I will. Thank you."

Deep in thought, he ate slowly and was relieved when the females and pups left the cave to bathe. It was much easier to function when *she* wasn't around. He finished his meal slowly, pushed the plate away from the edge of the table then looked at Zane.

The man's knee rubbed his. "Have you had enough, Cole? I thought we might want to visit the stream before turning in for the night."

"The others are down there," Cole objected. He envisioned Shira standing below the cool trickling water of the cascade, her round, brown nipples erect against firm, white breasts. His cock pulsed merely imagining her naked in the water. If he were actually to see her... He inhaled.

"They're coming back already. Look." Zane nodded towards the cave entrance. Four females, each carrying an exhausted but clean pup, traipsed through the den. "They washed up quickly. Those pups have had it. I bet they'll sleep well into tomorrow."

"Yes, I imagine they will." Cole watched them pass, making brief eye contact with Shira. The clean gown she wore was barely long enough to cover her bum and clung to her curves in a most exciting way. A sleeping Hani covered her upper half. Her legs under the fabric caught his eye. He stared at the tantalising 'V' between them as she approached him and the sway of her full hips when she passed and walked on.

Shira glanced back at him over her shoulder then looked away.

Cole swallowed.

"What do you say?" Zane leaned close, speaking into his ear. "A dip in the fresh water sound good?"

"Yes." Cole stood, gathering his bearings. "It sounds very good." Walking out, he couldn't help looking back towards the alcove where the women would sleep. Shira had laid Hani down and was preparing to settle herself in for the night. Her breasts swung back and forth as she climbed onto the pile of fur bedding set up for her.

Cole was mesmerised. The thought of burying his face between those fleshy mounds was all-encompassing, and he couldn't look away.

"Would you prefer that?" Zane murmured.

Cole turned to face Zane. "What?"

Zane smiled. "If you're too tired to bathe, I could give you a back rub in your den right now. If you'd prefer that."

"No, let's get out of here." Cole grabbed Zane's arm and led him down to the river.

Chapter Three

Cole turned his face upwards into the stream of water. Cool and refreshing, it helped clear his head now that Shira was out of sight. He'd never experienced such a thing and, at that moment, he needed to put it from his mind. He stepped back, shook his head and inhaled deeply.

Zane dropped to his knees before him and grasped both buttocks in his hands. "I've wanted to do this all day." He nuzzled Cole's erection and the heavy ball sac that hung beneath. "Come to me, you gorgeous beast."

"Whatever you say." Cole thrust his groin forward, allowing his cock to disappear down Zane's throat. "Oh, yeah."

Zane didn't speak again, just devoured Cole with an intensity that took Cole's breath. Hands gripped Cole's arse firmly, keeping their bodies close. Sucking and swallowing, Zane brought Cole to the point of insatiable need.

Cole's balls churned and drew up. His lover's mouth felt exquisite, but he had something more in mind for their coupling. "Wait." He pressed Zane back.

"Mmm, so close. Let me taste you. I want your cum flowing down my throat."

"Not yet." Cole dragged Zane to his feet. "My turn to play. Lean against the rocks."

Zane did as instructed. Facing Cole, he propped his elbows on the ledge behind him for support.

Cole kissed his way down the tanned, muscular body, listening for any and all reaction from the man. He stopped to lick each flat nipple before dipping lower, enthralled by the soft sighs and gasps of pleasure he caused. He nuzzled the smooth abdomen and moved lower yet to bury his face in the nest of light, curly hair. "Oh, yes. My turn to enjoy."

Zane's erection stood out from his body, full and thick, a drop of pre-cum glistening on the slit. Cole wasted no time before flicking it off with his tongue. The standing man groaned, and Cole smiled.

"See the torture I endured?" Like a hungry pup, he licked and teased the cock to produce another creamy pearl then laved his tongue over it smoothly.

"No more teasing!" Zane thrust his hips forward. "Take it all."

"If that's what you want." Eagerly, Cole covered the shaft with his mouth and moved slowly to swallow every inch. His face again nestled in the mat of pubic hair, he groaned. Nuzzling his nose there, he inhaled the musky scent of him.

Zane pulled back and murmured huskily, "Oh, yes. Yes!"

Cole held his lover's thighs, encouraging him with gentle pressure to fuck his face for as long as he liked. He adored the desperate plunging of a rampant cock into his mouth. The soft pressing of the firm, round balls rubbing against his chin made him hungry for more. The urge to fuck was strong, the act of receiving it, whether in the arse or in the mouth, was even stronger.

He relaxed his throat muscles and enjoyed the full, pulsing shaft that filled his mouth. When Zane's ball sac tightened, Cole felt it against his lower lip and knew the man's climax was near. He steadied himself for the onslaught of creamy, warm fluid.

"Fuck!" Zane cried out, his body convulsing as he emptied down Cole's willing throat.

Cole held him tight, swallowing frantically and taking all his lover had to offer before finally withdrawing. "Mmm, you do taste good. Sorry I denied you the same pleasure. But I've got other plans for my nice, hard cock."

"Please." Zane spread his legs and lifted one knee to his chest.

Zane's dark rosebud appeared before Cole, who leaned in to nuzzle it. He licked around the puckered opening then forced his tongue past the tight, outer ring. He pressed in as deeply as possible before pulling out. "Now, that tastes good. I'd love to stay longer, but my erection might burst if I continue to deny it."

"We wouldn't want that." Zane eyed him lustily.

Cole glanced around quickly. "Over there," he motioned to a smooth, moss-covered, flat rock. "On your back."

Zane scrambled to oblige.

Kneeling over him, Cole spread the strong thighs and kneaded the flesh. He pressed the man's legs upwards, his knees to his chest, again exposing the desired target. "Nice." He slid one hand smoothly over the soft, fleshy arse before raising his arm and sharply slapping one cheek.

Zane grunted.

Smiling, Cole caressed the reddened flesh. He'd caught his lover off-guard, and that made it even more fun. He saw Zane's cock twitch and thicken, there was no doubt he enjoyed it, too. Without speaking, he quickly spanked the other cheek then landed a third slap directly in the middle over the rose-coloured anus.

"Please," Zane mumbled, almost incoherently.

"Please what, my handsome one?"

Zane looked him in the eye. His lust, so recently slaked, had risen again and turned to carnal desperation. "Please fuck me."

Cole grinned with pleasure. Spreading the man's thighs even wider, he shifted between them. He stroked his own shaft firmly, squeezing pre-cum out for lubrication. He nudged the tip of his cock against Zane's hole and rubbed it around then, with a finger, he worked in the slickness.

"More." Zane bucked his hips.

"It's coming, greedy boy. Let me stretch you properly, first." Cole added a second finger and worked it around, tugging carefully. He took his time, gently stretching his lover's hole, while he toyed with the plump ball sac and rapidly rising cock. Each groan was like music to his ears, every squirming push towards his hand, the dance he craved seeing. When three fingers slid in and out easily, he returned his cock into place. "There we go. I won't bother to ask if you're ready for this. Your bum is burning with red heat, and your cock is thick again. You're ready. More than ready." He pressed the tip in, gritting his teeth at the delicious pressure around him.

"Yes, ready." Zane reached for Cole's arms as if searching desperately for something to hang onto.

Cole's shaft penetrated the tight hole, inch-by-inch and, once fully seated, both men groaned. Such an exquisite feeling, his cock enveloped in velvety tightness. Cole hated to move.

"More!" Zane muttered, raising his groin.

"You're in such a rush." Cole leaned down and kissed him, his tongue searching Zane's mouth unhurriedly. When he had to take a breath, he backed away and whispered, "I want it slow. Let's make it last all night."

Zane gritted his teeth. "I want it hard and fast, my teasing lover. When you spank me like that, I instantly grow hard. All I want is to be fucked. The devil with making it last all night. We can do other things in your bed back at the den. Right now, *I need you to fuck me!*"

Cole chuckled and pulled his cock out until the outer ring held just the tip. He slammed it back in, jolting both their systems and driving a gasp from his lover.

Zane's eyes rolled back in his head.

Summoning all his strength, Cole pummelled the taut body below his until they were both sweating. His climax loomed, another few strokes and he'd let loose. "Soon," he whispered.

Zane grabbed his own shaft and pumped it back and forth between their stomachs. His movements became strained, his strokes desperate, and when he tensed, Cole knew he was there.

"Now!" Zane moaned and exploded. Ribbons of creamy seed splattered both their chests.

Cole gave in to the sensations and let his own climax free. Shuddering, his body on fire from the intensity of it all, he exploded. A gut-wrenching sob reached his ears, just as his first spasm struck, sending a geyser of cum deep into his lover's arse. He held himself in deep, digging his toes into the gravel at the bottom of the river to remain embedded in the hot, silken glove. He thrust again, sending a second hot gush of cum deep into Zane's rectum and causing him to clench. He clung to Zane and rode it out then collapsed over him, panting as if he'd run a race.

"That was perfect," Zane finally whispered.

Burying his face in the man's neck, Cole inhaled deeply of his rich, masculine scent. The more time they spent together, the more he felt their connection growing. That hadn't been comfortable for him at first. He'd always preferred the casual, no-strings approach to sex. But suddenly, being here, wrapped between Zane's muscular thighs and held in his arms, felt right and good. "Perfect," he agreed.

Zane ran a hand down his back and cupped Cole's arse. "Don't move. You feel too good right there."

Cole ground himself against Zane. It did feel good. In fact, he couldn't imagine anything better.

Unbidden, the image of Shira's naked breasts popped into his head. He envisioned sucking the full, ripe tits, felt himself driving his cock deep into her slick pussy. Her eyes would stare at him and, if he dared look back, he'd be drawn into the deep, blue pools of emotion.

He shook his head guiltily, stopping only when Zane reached for him and drew him into a kiss.

* * * *

Later, while the rest of the pack slept, a confused Cole sat alone in the pack's main chamber, gazing into the fire. Zane lay deeply asleep on Cole's furs, the picture of peace. For a while, he'd lain, watching him, wondering at his feelings for the beautiful white-haired man and where the woman came into things. Finally, he had to leave or risk waking Zane with his tossing and turning. Pulling on his trousers, he'd wandered into the big chamber.

Feeding the embers with some of the dried wood piled just outside, he sat looking into the flame. The tryst at the river had been amazing. Zane excited him like none other had, and he wondered if perhaps he'd found his true mate. The man made him feel special in so many ways. *Do I deserve such a thing?*

As soon as he recalled how their lovemaking had ended, he also envisioned Shira. Red curls blowing in the wind, her lovely curves a feast for the senses, and even though he'd never laid eyes on her more intimate parts, he couldn't help but wonder if her pubes were as auburn as the hair on her head. His stomach lurched. The front of his trousers felt tight against the growing erection inside.

He wondered who the father of the pups was. Thinking of her with another male cooled his ardour somewhat and confused him even more. He craved Zane, as he'd never craved another. Yet he couldn't seem to shake thoughts of the glorious redhead from his mind.

Frustrated and angry with himself, he climbed to his feet and paced around the fire pit, kicking at small bits of wood that had escaped the flame. The talisman heated a patch on his thigh right through his pants, reminding him of yet one more dilemma with which he had to deal, and soon. He reached into his pocket, drew out the golden filigree and gazed at the blood red stone cradled inside. He wanted to fling it away. He wanted to be free and uncaring, but he knew, deep down, that part of his life was over. He just had to admit it.

"Cole." A soft voice startled him.

He thrust the talisman back into its nesting place. Spinning towards the sound, he couldn't help but smile. It was Shira, dressed in a clean night shift, her breasts straining against the top, her hips pulling the middle section tight across her tummy, and the hem just barely covering her pubes. Below, she was barefoot. In the firelight, she was gorgeous.

His guilt returned, but he pushed it aside. "Yes, what is it? Are you all right?" he asked in a rush.

She took a few steps closer and raised her hand. "Everything's fine. I couldn't sleep. I saw you and just wanted to thank you for insisting we come." She stopped a mere pace away, close enough for him to see the twinkle in her beautiful, blue eyes.

"Come and sit with me by the fire," he held out a hand to her. When she took it, a tingle ran up his arm.

She must have felt something, too, for she glanced down then up into his eyes, her mouth a round 'O' of surprise. Blinking, she closed her mouth and shivered. "I'd like that."

He guided her to the place he'd just vacated and held her hand until she was seated, her back to the bench. Joining her, he was afraid to sit too close, afraid the feelings he'd been fighting would overcome him. He sat with his knees wide and his ankles crossed. Leaning forward, he poked a stick into the flames.

"Are the pups settled all right?" he asked hesitantly. He wanted to be direct, to ask about their father, but didn't want to push her. She'd had too much happen to her over the last few days, and he didn't want to add to her burden of grief.

"They're fine," she whispered then sighed. "Pups adjust fast to just about anything. They needed food, but when that need was satisfied, their little world was good." She gazed at the far wall, her eyes becoming unfocused, as if she saw a much different vista.

Cole watched her, ached to comfort her, but was unsure how she'd take it. So many issues he didn't know about. *How can I approach her? How can I ask her to stay?*

He blinked at his thoughts. Guilt tore at him. Zane—he was growing to love the man. What was happening to him?

He shifted and realised his cock was again erect, the tip pressing against the waistband of his trousers. Placing the palm of his hand against the bulge, he tried to will the stiffness away, with no luck. It throbbed. Stifling a groan, he knew he was in trouble when he turned and saw her smiling at him. Her gaze went from his eyes to where his hand rested on his crotch.

"You seem to be in difficulty. Would you like me to leave?" She winked and made as if to rise.

"No." He reached out and took her by the arm, urging her to remain seated. The last thing he wanted was for her to leave. He was totally captivated by her. "Damn."

Shira settled back down, her hand brushing the outside of his thigh. Another jolt of tingling pleasure travelled from there, upwards. His cock twitched.

"Are you all right?" she asked, her eyes twinkling with laughter.

He looked at her, opened his mouth to say something brilliant, but all that came out was a rush of air accompanying a soft grunt. He was speechless, dumb with frustration. Closing his mouth, he took a deep breath and strained to calm himself. He tried again, with better results. "I'm fine. I don't want to upset you, but I…"

"Upset me? What's wrong?" She cocked her head and looked at him, obviously mystified. "Why would you upset me?"

"Nothing, I promise. It's just that you've been through so much. You've lost your pack, your mate…" He let that go for a moment, hoping she'd jump in and say something. She didn't, so he went on. "Only you and Meghan and the pups survived. That's got to weigh heavily on you."

Her eyes darkened, and he knew she was remembering the horror of those events. "Yes, it was awful. The pups saw it all. The poor babes."

"Yes, but you saved them. Your pups, I mean." There, he'd said it, and now he waited.

She was in no hurry to relieve his discomfort or was simply so lost in her thoughts his words didn't connect for a moment. Finally, she shuddered, her eyes took on a more animated look, and she replied, "We saved each other. I think if it hadn't been for the pups, Meghan and I would have gone back into the flames. Our families...everyone we loved, our homes, are all gone." A tear trickled its way down her cheek.

He wiped it away with the tip of his finger. "You haven't lost it all. The pups, your friend...or sister. Meghan."

"Meghan isn't my sister. She was our pack leader's chosen. Those are her pups."

Cole's heart skipped a beat. He wanted to whoop his pleasure, but fought down the urge. Still, he needed to know if she had been mated to someone. Was she in mourning?

Feeling as if there were no easy way, he simply blurted it out. "And you? Did you lose a mate? Pups?"

When he saw her eyes brimming with tears, he pulled her into his arms. He'd said too much. Pushed her too hard. He wanted to kick himself for being such a fool.

Her body shook as she cried for her dead. Tears she probably should have shed days ago trickled down his chest. He held her and stroked her and was about as uncomfortable as a male could be, but he willingly shared her sorrow as best as he could. Her hair smelled of cedar and fresh air, and he pressed his face into the soft abundance of it. Sliding his hand over her back, he felt her cringe when he touched the left side. The burns she'd been unwilling to admit to, he assumed, and moved his hand away.

"Now, now, it's all right. You're here, now, and the pups will be fine. So will you, if you stay with us. You'll fit in, I know you will. And redheads are special." He mumbled nonsense, just words to calm her and ease the pain she endured. He felt her breasts pressing against his chest, the nipples like small pebbles dragging across his skin as she moved. He inhaled deeply and felt light-headed. Her scent made it hard to concentrate. She was driving him wild, and he wanted to touch her intimately, take her, but he dared not. Not yet.

His erection was back full force, and he fervently hoped she wouldn't notice. He twisted to the side, pulling her across his lap. Her arms draped around his neck, and again he inhaled the sexy smell of her. Woman scent, wolf bitch, and he wanted her desperately.

He kissed her hair, lightly, timidly, unsure of her desire for him yet unable to control the need to comfort her. Carefully, he slipped a hand around to her belly, moved it upwards until it bumped into the under-curve of her breast. There it stayed, gently touching the soft yet firm mound, giving him about as much pleasure as he could stand, and hopefully her as well. He caught the new smell, her arousal, a moment later, and smiled into her hair.

Shira's sobs eased, slowly fading until she simply sat cradled in his arms, hers still wrapped around him. Her lips were pressed to his neck. He felt them there, soft, luscious, wet.

"I'm glad you're here," he whispered into her hair. He felt breathless. His heart was beating so fast, it must have made quite a racket in her head.

"I'm glad we came, too." Her lips brushed his chest, tickled him in a way that made him shiver and want more. "I was so afraid we'd die out there." She sobbed again, but only one time.

"We'd have found you. If not that day, then when we went to bury our tribal leader and his mate." He flashed on the remains of Gar and Ruby. How sad it was that they'd gone, but how right that they'd been together when it happened.

"But it was you who found us, and you who convinced me to come here."

"Yes, it was. I'm glad it was."

"I don't have a mate, Cole. I was never attracted to the males of our pack." She pulled her face from his chest and tilted her head back. Their eyes met and locked. "The sex was always good, but I never stayed with anyone."

"Well, perhaps you'll find someone here."

Blinking away her tears, she looked up at him and tried on a smile. "Maybe I will."

He leaned towards her and kissed her, gently, tentatively. Her lips were soft and wet, and when he ran his tongue along the seam joining top lip to bottom, they parted, allowing him entrance. He ran his tongue across her teeth, savoured the sleepy taste of her mouth and was breathless in moments.

Pulling back, Cole looked into her eyes, trying to spot any hesitancy or fear and finding none. He wanted her, desperately, and from the hungry look on her face, she felt the same about him. With his hands still on her, he twisted her around until she lay across his lap, his erection stabbing into her back. He hoped he wasn't hurting her, dragging himself across the painful burn that was still healing. The med powder was good, but it seemed the injury had been more serious than he'd thought.

She twisted a little but settled back down, her arm once more going around his neck. "Come here and kiss me." Her voice was harsh with desire.

"Hey, we're rushing an awful lot, here. Are you sure you wouldn't rather wait for—"

She didn't let him finish but simply pulled his mouth down to hers. Her breath on his cheek came an instant before her lips touched his. Her tongue flashed out, slid across then thrust between them and sank eagerly inside. As she stroked the sides of his tongue with hers, they were soon lost in the steamy world of sex and pleasure. The gentle sucking progressed to more aggressive nipping and chewing. His hands wandered over her, tugging at the top of her shift, opening it to allow his fingers to stray inside.

Blood pounded in his veins, and his body ached with the need to move, to thrust into her. He knew his wolfen self was very close to the surface.

She turned to face him, her knees straddling his thighs. She straightened up, thrusting her chest out, and moved her hands to the hem of the shift. With her eyes locked on his, she slowly pulled the nightdress up, baring the tiny auburn thatch of pubic hair he'd wondered about only minutes before. The roundness of her hips drew him closer, and, as she pulled the shift higher, he slid his hands over her hot flesh.

She teased him then, sliding her nakedness against him but refusing to reveal her tits. He desperately wanted to worship them with his teeth and lips. The taut flesh of her belly slid across his chest, and she lifted the hem a hand span higher, showing him just the under-curve of each luscious mound.

His mouth watered, and he couldn't control the grunt of pleasure he felt as her body moved against him. His cock strained against his trousers, aching to be free. "You're gorgeous. Let me love you," he crooned, his blood boiling with need.

"And you are driving me crazy," she whimpered and finally whipped her shift off. Tossing it across the bench, she arched her body away from him, displaying her beauty.

"So lovely, so soft. You fire me, woman." His voice was a throaty growl. He slipped one hand over her arse and up her back, pulling it away when he saw her cringed. *The burn, damn!* More carefully, he caressed her spine and the soft curves of her back and shoulders. "Let me pleasure you. Please, let me."

Shira cupped his face in her small hands and lifted his chin so he had to look her in the eyes. "You can take what you want."

"Yes, I can. But I only want what's given freely." He sat forward and, taking her weight in his hands, he lowered her to the floor. "Would you like a pelt? I can get one from my room."

"No, just you. Just you." Her words came in soft pants, and she couldn't seem to make her body be still. Her hips moved, and her legs flexed.

Smiling, he looked around for something on which to lay her. Spotting an old pelt the pups used for playing on, he jumped up and fetched it. He tossed it on the floor beside her and watched her shift onto it. Then he took his time pulling off his trousers. What was good for the gander was good for the goose, or in this case, the bitch wolf. After unfastening them, he eased his thumbs into the waistband and wriggled them down over his hips. He twisted around and looked at her over his shoulder, smiling when he saw her eyes were glued to his backside.

"Ah, you like a man's arse," he teased, drawing his hands around and running them over the smooth muscles of his bum.

"Yes, I like a man's body. All of it." She sat up and held out a hand for him, but he quickly stepped out of her reach.

"Good." He slid his trousers off. When his erection sprang free, he couldn't control a sigh of pleasure.

"I want to see you." Shira again reached for him.

"You will. Patience, my girl." He turned and pushed his trousers down further, bending forward, covering himself as he forced each side over the foot. When he rose and tossed the pants aside, he allowed her to see him naked for the first time.

"You're beautiful, Cole."

He chuckled and knelt before her. "'Beautiful' isn't exactly a masculine thing to call a male."

"But you are." She slid a hand over his chest, took a nipple between her finger and thumb and squeezed the hard, little nubbin until he groaned. Her other hand moved lower, gripping his erection firmly at the base. "And this is beautiful, too."

His cock pulsed, and he gritted his teeth to keep from thrusting into her hand. Control, he strained for it, thought of a dozen things to keep from driving forward. Sweat trickled down his back and from under his arms. He shuddered. When she tightened her fist, he gasped, "Keep it up and you'll make me shoot."

She looked up at him, feigned innocence on her flushed face. "Me? How could I make you do anything you don't want to do?"

"Womanly wiles, your hand, maybe your mouth, I can think of a dozen ways." He pulled back, drawing his cock from her grasp. "I actually have something in mind."

He gazed at the two luscious mounds of flesh before lowering his mouth to the perfect brown nipple of the first. It tightened under his lips, hardening into a firm nub. He grazed it with his teeth and sucked it deeply into his mouth.

Shira moaned and arched her back, offering him more.

A low growl rumbled in the back of his throat as he suckled her, kneading the flesh with his hand. When that nipple was cone-shaped, he switched sides, rolling the first between his thumb and forefinger.

He lavished the same treatment on her second lovely tit, licking and sucking until he thought his cock might burst without ever being touched. He'd never experienced such pleasure with a female before, and adored basking in the fleshy differences between her body and Zane's.

Zane. The thought hit him like a ton of bricks. How could he be there with Shira when, just hours earlier, he'd been in Zane's arms? Zane had pleased him like no one ever had. Yet, here he was, seeking out another person to fuck.

Not just fuck. Shira beckoned him, instinctively it seemed, from somewhere on another level. He couldn't explain it any more than he could stop it. He had to have her, yearned to explore her in every possible way.

He squeezed both breasts, the soft flesh bulging out between his fingers in small mounds, then reluctantly left them to move on. He traced a line of kisses down her stomach until he reached the V-shaped apex of her legs. Pushing them apart, he settled onto his stomach between her thighs and leaned forward to examine her femininity much closer.

The scent of her arousal was strong, and he breathed it in deeply, hungrily. Carefully parting the sparse covering of shiny, red hair, he pulled her fleshy, outer lips apart. Unable simply to look for a moment longer, he dipped in his tongue and dragged it across one smooth, wet fold.

Shira gasped, and her hips twitched.

He grinned at her reaction and dived in again, wanting to make her really squirm. He spread her more fully and exposed the pink button nestled between her nether lips. With the tip of his tongue, Cole flicked her clitoris and enjoyed the taste of her musky essence. It nearly drove him wild, and he buried his face in her pussy, seeking more.

"Oh, yes!" Her thighs twitched under his hands, the rest of her body tensing as he delved deeper.

When he inserted his tongue into her velvety, slick channel, her muscles contracted around him. He thrust in, again and again, thinking about nothing more than tasting as much of her as possible and driving her to new heights of pleasure. When he was at the deepest point, tongue fully extended and chin pressed against her body, she cried out with an earthy, guttural moan. Rocking with orgasm, her hips rose so fast, if he hadn't been holding on tight, she'd have dislodged him for sure. Clutching her body to his face, he kept up his pace, hoping to prolong the pleasure. *The first of many at my hand,* he thought with satisfaction, *or rather, my mouth.*

Shira quivered for long moments before reaching down and running a hand through his hair. "Beautiful," she murmured.

He covered her pussy and inner thighs with tiny kisses then worked his way up her body. His cock was painfully rigid, and he knew from his limited experience that sex with a well-lubricated female didn't require as much preparation as he was used to. Reaching between them, he grasped his shaft and guided it home.

Shira's arms slid around his neck, her fingers playing over his shoulders and back with a light touch. She adjusted her hips, allowing him to sink in fully, and wrapped her legs tightly around his arse.

They gazed into each other's eyes as Cole began a series of slow thrusts, designed to drive them both insane. He leaned forward and kissed her hungrily, their tongues batting back and forth.

It felt so different, being in the arms of a shapely female. Her body was pliant and soft against his, not muscular and solid like the males he was so used to mounting. The females he'd mated with as a wolf were an entirely different matter. In animal form, whether he was with a male or female, fucking was pure, carnal, physical activity. He loved it, no doubt about that, but it was something so entirely dissimilar, the two acts could barely be compared.

With his chest pressed against Shira's flattened breasts and his cock embedded as deeply inside her as possible, Cole ground his hips into hers. Shira clung to his neck, and her body quivered in that special way he was learning signified her orgasm.

"Yes!" she growled in his ear.

Cole clutched her back and groaned his release, sending loads of warm cum shooting deep inside her. The intensity of each shuddering release took his breath. Shira groped for his face, her lips finding his for a deep, hungry kiss that brought it back. He gasped for air and kissed her, until it seemed they were breathing for each other.

Chapter Four

When Cole stopped shuddering, and his breathing returned to something approaching normal, he grasped Shira's arse and pulled her firmly against him. He flipped them over so she was on top, yet he remained planted deep inside her.

"Neat trick." She sat up just enough to allow her breasts to bob in his face.

He nipped playfully at each tit then settled back, his hands resting comfortably on her thighs. "I wanted to get you off your back. I don't know why you're being so stoic. I know you must have a hell of a burn there."

"It's getting better." She squirmed, just talking about it.

"If it's not better by tomorrow, I'll apply more of the medicinal powders. It shouldn't take that long to heal."

Shira leaned down again and kissed him tenderly on his lips. "Thank you. So...tonight you loved me tenderly, as a man cherishes a woman. Tomorrow we might shift to wolves, and I'll let you chase me down to the river and mount me like the beasts we both are." Her eyes twinkled. "Doesn't that sound like fun?"

Cole laid a palm against her face. "It does. Not that anything could beat the fun we've had here, tonight." He bucked his hips, jostling her.

She smiled. "Thank you, Cole. Thank you for making me feel alive again." She pushed on his abdomen, allowing his cock to slip from her pussy. Standing up, she reached for her night shift and glanced to the side of the den for a moment before looking at him one last time. "Good night. See you tomorrow."

"Don't go!" He wove his fingers behind his head.

She gazed to the side once again then back at him. She blew him a kiss before returning to the alcove she shared with the other females and pups.

Cole watched her go, inhaling deeply then slowly letting the air out. He was just getting started. His cock was half-erect again. He could have gone on all night.

A noise made him jump, and he looked in the direction he'd seen her gaze, towards his sleeping alcove. Zane stood in the doorway, but before they made eye contact, the blond man backed away.

"Zane!" Cole leapt to his feet. He made sure the fire was contained then grabbed his clothes before hurrying into the small alcove he called home.

To his surprise, Zane appeared to be asleep on the bed of furs, exactly where Cole had left him.

Cole knelt next to him and, leaning forward, spoke softly into his ear. "Are you awake?"

The white-haired man didn't stir.

"Zane." Cole couldn't believe he really was asleep. Or perhaps all he'd seen was a vision of Zane, borne of guilt.

How could he have just lain with Shira only hours after being with Zane? How could he be so damn confused?

Cole flopped onto his side of the bed and stared at the gorgeous, kind-hearted man sleeping there. He'd made a mistake. He'd always been inclined to take a male lover, and he fully expected to choose a male mate. Zane trusted him and had opened his heart to him. Cole had betrayed that and had stomped Zane's heart into the ground. He was a dog, a filthy, mangy creature who didn't deserve the trust of such a good man. Rolling over, he threw his arms over his head and sought sleep. A sleep, that when it finally came, was filled with haunting visions of both Zane and Shira calling to him.

* * * *

Waking before Zane in the darkness of pre-dawn, Cole slipped quietly from the bed. He couldn't face him yet. He dressed in a simple loincloth, not intending to remain in human form for long, and left the alcove.

When he stepped into the central room of the den, memories flooded his senses of being with Shira the night before. He didn't want to face her, either. For some damn reason, he wasn't his normal self around the sexy she-wolf. *More like putty in her hands,* he thought wryly. Confused and not particularly proud of himself, he grabbed a strip of jerky and headed out the front entrance of the cave.

Ulric was there, lacing his boots in preparation for travel. "Morning, Cole."

"Ulric," he acknowledged. "It's still dark. You two setting off already?"

"As soon as Kaleb returns. He's gathering supplies and a special shroud cloth."

"That'll be good. I gave Kaleb detailed instructions about where to find the bodies." He moved around Ulric, preparing to set out on a small journey himself.

"Cole." Ulric grabbed his arm. "Kaleb told me you have the talisman."

"I do." He'd hidden it in his sleeping alcove, still unwilling to put it around his neck.

Ulric's smile was strained and not particularly friendly. "He seems to think you're a good choice to be our new tribal leader. I'm not convinced I agree with him."

"Oh?" *I'm not convinced of it, either.* He wouldn't admit that to Ulric, though. His mentor's mate had always treated him kindly, but the grip Ulric had on Cole's arm felt anything but easy-going or friendly.

"Tala, as Gar's sole surviving offspring, thinks the amulet might belong to her. She wonders why no one has seen it but you. I question that as well."

Cole raised his eyebrows. "Indeed? You'd like to see Tala leading the tribe?"

Ulric chuckled. "Not hardly. Tala is a fine female, I suppose, although I've never had much use for bitches. No, I believe there are others in the pack better suited to the task. "

"You, I presume?"

The older man smiled again. "Me or Kaleb. Our hearts beat as one. Either of us has the maturity and wisdom required to fulfil the duties of a tribal leader."

"Which I don't." Cole's ire grew as he talked to Ulric. Kaleb hadn't indicated he felt that way the previous night.

He'd almost encouraged Cole to accept the amulet. Perhaps the mated males' hearts beat as one, but apparently, they were of separate minds.

"If you did, would Kaleb and I be retracing your steps to take care of Gar and Ruby's remains? You should have handled that when you found them."

Guilt pierced Cole to the quick, but he faced Ulric stubbornly. "Zane and I had many responsibilities on our journey. Our leader was dead. And since we didn't have shrouds with us, I thought it best to leave them for others to see to while I brought the talisman back to the clan."

Ulric's eyes flashed. "You're not the tribe's leader yet, young one with the smart mouth. I'll let this go for now out of respect for Kaleb. He feels some crazy loyalty to you. But it's not over. Nothing's been decided until the amulet's been presented to the pack, so we can see for our own eyes. Remember that."

"Yes, sir. And, may I remind you, it will be the talisman that chooses, not you or Tala or anyone else." Cole glared at him for a moment before he pulled his arm free and, turning on his heel, stormed off. For a moment, he thought he should return to his den and get the amulet. It might not be prudent to let it out of his hands. Glancing back, he spotted Shira at the entrance to the cave, watching him.

In his current mood, he still wasn't prepared to face her or, worse yet, Zane. Cole hurried off into the brush where he could be alone and dropped to his hands and knees.

Shifting from man to wolf took mere minutes, but the stabbing pain never failed to surprise him, and the following pleasure always excited him. He arched his back, the muscles along his spine shifted, and the torment turned to sweet bliss. His bones condensed, thickened, while his arms extended, and his fingers cramped, morphing into small pads.

Cole shuddered as his spine realigned itself. He groaned with both pleasure and torment as his nose elongated and ears drew up on top of his head. Claws formed where nail beds once lay. Fur sprouted from skin, a thick, sleek, grey-brown pelt. His cock and balls flattened against his body, while a tail emerged and grew above his arse.

He stretched, revelling in his reborn shape. He loved the purely animalistic feel that being a wolf gave him, and he fought back the urge to howl. *Much too close to the den for that.* Shaking himself, he took off, loping at a sprinter's pace through the forest and massive, black-tinged trees.

It felt wonderful to move, to breathe and to be at peace with nature and his surroundings. If he were a true wolf, and not a changeling, he wouldn't have to worry about his feelings. Trust, betrayal, lust and longing were part of the human world. Wolves simply existed. Took action when necessary and did what needed to be done without discussing every fucking thing to the smallest detail.

There was a social hierarchy, and each pack was ruled by the breeding pair. Gar and Ruby had been prolific, producing many offspring in their time. Yet, Tala was their only surviving heir, the others having fallen ill and died or been killed by accident over the years. As age crept up on the leader and his mate, by consent, Yive and Theron became the breeding pair. But Theron, although strong of body, was weak of spirit, and the first wolf to challenge him aggressively would likely chase him off. Cole had never been interested in dominance or any of the responsibilities that came with it, until very recently.

Suddenly, for some unknown reason, he thought about it all the time.

Gar might have stepped aside as breeding pack leader, but he continued to carry the talisman, and ruled the tribe with wisdom and kindness. He'd told Cole the story of their ancestors, how the amulet had saved the changelings from constant bloodshed and turmoil. How the tribes had been formed from the multitude of family clans and packs of each of the three changeling nations.

In those years, and the hundreds previous, the changeling tribes had been at war within themselves. Tearing each other apart, each small family group had seemed to need more territory and game. Their numbers rose and fell at alarming rates. Not only wolf packs were affected, but the cougars and bears, as well. Then Cato, of the cougar clan, had discovered the secret of the amulets. He kept one for the cougars, placed a second where the bears would find it, then left a third for the wolves.

Xeno, the first wolf to hold the brilliant red talisman, had been a strong, hulking creature, possibly more powerful in legend than he had been in life. His mate and one breeding partner, Mesa, bore him many offspring during their lives together. Hunting one day, Xeno had discovered the amulet of ornate gold filigree encasing the sparkling red stone. Upon further inspection, he'd seen the delicate gold was twisted into the shape of a wolf's head.

The gem had warmed Xeno's palm and planted some unusual thoughts in his head. A plan had formed that could set in motion a way to end the conflict—a way to live in peace for all the clans and all three of the tribes. Each of three stones had been given to the race indicated by the delicate threads of gold. Among those races, or tribes, only one could hold the talisman. That one must have a life-mate who would stand with him through everything. He must also have the good of all the family clans of his breed in his heart. Only those the amulet deemed worthy could hold the charm, and only those who were mated for life could keep it for long.

Xeno had accepted the duty proudly, restoring peace and honour to the wolfen packs. Mesa, his strong, wise mate, had aided him, and the tribes soon found peace. There had been harmony for many generations since, with the talismans going to new owners when the old passed on.

Now, Cole had possession of the wolfen tribe's powerful, red stone, and the worry of what to do with it.

He raced through the woods, trying to outrun his thoughts and problems. Deep in his heart, he knew it wouldn't work, but it felt blissfully good to try.

The wind ruffled the fur along his back, the rocks dug into the soft areas between his pads. To his left, he watched a rabbit scurry into the underbrush and, for an instant, he thought of racing after it. *Fresh meat,* he thought, and his mouth filled with saliva. Running free, responsibilities of any kind the farthest thing from his thoughts, he rejoiced in the play of his muscles moving easily as he distanced himself from the pack.

He turned and headed for the deep forest. The further he ran, the less he saw of the fire's damage, until finally he came to a stream that was pristine and bordered by waves of emerald green herbage. He threw himself to his back in the grass, rolling around like a pup. The gentle whisperings of the stream called to him, reminding him of his thirst. The run had dried his mouth, and he eagerly lapped up the clear liquid while watching small fish dart away.

After he drank his fill, he went to the nearest tree and lifted his leg, sending a stream of piss to its base. Marking his territory was something Gar had taught him to do years ago. Done, he turned his back and kicked up dirt, spraying the tree with the moist loam.

Gar, the great wolf who'd led the tribe for longer than Cole had been alive. How could anyone step into his role? How could *Cole*?

Thrusting the thought away, he sauntered along the bank of the stream. He'd been there before, months ago, with a young man from a nearby pack who'd bumped into him while they were both hunting. The game trail had quickly led to a much more pleasurable afternoon and evening of blissful male-on-male sex. They'd fucked as men, then they'd transformed and rutted as the beasts they both were, howling their pleasure. Hours later, when the moon had vanished behind the distant mountain range, they'd parted company and returned to their respective packs. Cole wondered idly if the raven-haired stud ever thought of him.

His focus returning to the present, he found himself daydreaming of Zane, his flaxen-haired lover. He'd never felt so in-tune with someone before. It centred him, made him feel as if he truly belonged to something important.

He reached a small, grassy ledge overlooking the stream and lay down, pondering the turn of events in his life.

Thinking of Zane made his blood race and his heart sing. He adored the man, but hadn't until that very moment realised how valuable Zane was. Learning about the man was more important than anything else at the moment. Pleasuring Zane, making sure he was cared for and happy, made Cole happy.

It was a strange feeling, and one he wanted more of.

He laid his chin on his paws and let his thoughts wander. Their last coupling had been amazing. The feel of the massive cock filling his mouth, the pulse of it as Zane's excitement soared, had his heart racing.

But just as he thought his mind was made up, the image of Shira popped into his head. Her soft femaleness sent a new flood of excitement straight to his groin. His cock thickened enough for the tip to peek out of its soft sheath and rub against the grass. His balls shifted. The mating had been incredible, her climax had made his heart soar. She, too, needed caring for, and it was a great pleasure for him to do so.

Confused, he climbed to his feet and paced back and forth, finally returning to the stream's edge. How could he care for them both?

The amulet came to mind, and he immediately wanted to feel it around his neck. *Insane*, he told himself. How would he ever benefit the tribe if he couldn't even settle his personal problems? The tribe needed someone much stronger than he was. Someone much wiser.

Maybe Ulric was right. Maybe he wasn't the right man-wolf to hold the talisman.

He was about to run when he spotted movement from the brush where he'd entered the clearing. He turned, facing whatever was approaching.

A moment later, a gorgeous, white wolf stepped from the woods. *Zane.*

Cole's heart skipped a beat, and his cock emerged another finger's width. Light headed, he took a step towards the magnificent beast, his tail wagging. He stopped and just looked at his lover, admiring the stance and the beast he was. Sleek fur lay flat along his sides, his chest was deep, his shoulders wide, and even through the snow-white pelt, Cole could see his haunch ripple with muscles.

Zane approached him, his head down, his arse high and his tail to one side. It was the look in the wolf's eyes that really took Cole's breath. Blue fire came to mind, and heat that could sear.

Cole took another step forward then inhaled, taking his mate's scent. Zane came the last few steps to him and gently, tenderly, licked his snout. *'My love.'*

Zane's thoughts were clear and made Cole shudder with pleasure. Cole eased along Zane's side, rubbing his own, sleek fur against that of his lover. He sniffed Zane's pelt and the base of the long, hefty tail sprouting from his backside.

Cole thought of the night before and cringed. Had Zane seen? Had it been a dream, his presence?

Zane yipped and tucked his rear end down, his tail between his legs. He scooted away. Another yip, and he pranced around Cole, nipping at him as he circled.

Cole stepped back, shocked, but quickly realised the wolf was playing. He leaped at Zane, shoulder down, head to the side, and managed to bowl him over. Rolling in the grass, the white beast barked before springing to his feet and racing for the woods. Cole went after him, all thoughts of his trouble fading as the two of them darted from one hiding spot to another, sniffing each other out then leaping off on another chase.

The morning passed that way, each of them taking a turn as the prey then becoming the predator when they were found. Zane, with his brilliant, white coat, was at a disadvantage but didn't seem to mind when Cole easily found him time after time.

Finally, winded and gasping for air, Cole turned and headed back to the stream. *'Come, my love, it's time to end our play.'*

Zane came out from under a half-rotted stump and trotted after him. Once they were at the streamside, Cole walked right into the water and leaned forward for a drink. The water was beautifully cold, and after a moment, he lowered himself to lie in a shallow pool. He shuddered when his belly touched down.

Zane stood beside him, his muzzle at water level and his pink tongue lapping up the refreshing liquid. Bits of grass clung to his fur, a smudge of dirt marred the silken, white expanse of his side, but he was the most amazing looking animal Cole could remember seeing.

His cock pulsed, yet he ignored it.

'We need to talk.'

Without raising his head, Zane replied, *'Yes, we do.'*

'Shift.'

Cole pulled himself to his feet and shook the water from his coat. He waited for Zane to finish drinking then ushered him to the shore. Side by side, they morphed.

A grunt of pain reached his ears just as his own guttural sob emerged from somewhere deep inside him. The realignment of his back and the stretching of his larger bones always signalled the beginning of the change. He saw stars for an instant, then the last trace of agony passed, followed by the sweet bliss of his musculature moving from one phase to another. His paws stretched, the claws sinking into the flesh, the nails flattening to become those of his human self. Hair receded into his skin, even his flesh altered, itched, like a legion of tiny fingers caressing him.

Turning his head, he watched Zane's spectacular coat vanish and the man's beautifully tanned flesh emerge. His gaze went from the broad shoulders and chest to his sides then further down. He watched his belly expand and contract with his breathing. And of course, that led to the hip and thigh then round to the curve of his arse.

Cole's excitement returned, and it took a great deal of effort to shift his gaze away. He needed to ask about last night. He needed to know what Zane thought of Shira. And most of all, he wanted to talk about the talisman, what it meant to him, to them both.

Strange, to finally think of himself as coupled — part of a mated pair.

"Are you all right?" Zane asked, his voice still rough from the change. "You look deep in thought."

Cole looked at him, adored the way his long, silken locks shimmered in the sun and slid across the beautifully tanned flesh when the wind caught it. His heart beat faster when he thought of actually being with this man for the rest of his life. How could he be so lucky? He knew he didn't deserve such an amazing mate.

"Yes, I'm okay." He rolled onto his side and held out an arm. The grass felt wonderfully cool against his back. "Come here, I want to tell you something."

Zane dropped into Cole's arms, resting his head against his shoulder. "And I have a confession to make."

"You do?" Thoughts of the lust-filled tryst he'd had with Shira last night came to mind. *I have my own confession to make.* He took a deep breath and said, "What have you to confess, my love?"

"You call me *love,* but maybe you won't when you hear what I have to say."

Cole shifted so he could look at Zane. "Tell me."

Zane closed his eyes, and for a moment, Cole wasn't sure he'd actually say whatever it was he needed to say.

When he opened them and looked into Cole's, he began. "It's about last night."

Cole's stomach did a flip-flop. It really had been Zane and not a guilt-derived vision standing at the entrance to the alcove. "Tell me, please."

"I saw you and Shira. I watched you fuck her, make love to her."

Cole felt as if he'd been kicked in the belly. What to say, how to go on? And more importantly, how could he make Zane understand he'd come to realise how much he loved him? "And?"

"And…" Zane let it fade.

If ever Cole had thought of eyes as being the windows to the soul, this was it. Pain, fear, longing and something more showed. He leaned forward and pressed his lips to the man's forehead. "And? Tell me, please."

"I'm afraid I'm going to lose you."

Cole lay back, waiting for him to go on. But the man didn't. Silence hung over them for long moments. Finally, realising Zane wasn't going to say anything else, Cole said, "Zane, my precious man-beast, you will never lose me." He decided to test the waters, toss his feelings out there and see what happened. "I love you."

Zane's eyes sparkled. "I love you, too, Cole. But when I saw you and Shira together, I thought..."

"You thought I wanted a mate who could give me young," Cole finished for the man. A shudder shook his arm, and he wanted to reach out and hold the man but didn't dare move. Not yet.

"Yes, I was so upset. That's why I left. And when you came to bed, I couldn't face you. I was afraid you'd ask me to leave."

When Cole rose up again and looked down at Zane, he saw tears in the man's eyes. "I was confused last night." He leaned forward and pressed his lips to Zane's. Gently, he slipped his tongue inside, tasting the salty sweetness of his lover's mouth. His cock pulsed and thickened, but again, he ignored it for the time being. Pulling his mouth away, he felt as if his heart was about to burst. Zane loved him. "I'm still confused about some things, but how I feel about you is not one of them. I love you, with all my heart. I've never felt like this before."

Zane opened his mouth as if to speak, but Cole pressed a finger to his lips. "No, let me finish what I have to say. It might make things clearer for us both."

Nodding, Zane lay back against his arm and simply looked up into Cole's eyes.

"I want to be sure you've got that. I love you. Nothing will change that. Okay?"

Zane nodded but didn't try to speak.

"Good. About Shira." He took a deep breath and hoped he could explain his feelings for her so Zane didn't feel threatened. Hell, he hoped he could explain how he felt so he understood it himself. "This is going to be much more difficult.

"I've never cared for a female before. To me, they've always just been there. Pack females were all right, and I know Gar wanted me to pair with Tala, but I just couldn't go there. I'm attracted to men much more than females. Fucking while they were in wolf form was amusing, easy, no ties, just animal fun. But when I saw Shira, something happened."

Zane tensed but didn't move or speak.

Cole felt it was safe to go on. "She's different, stronger, independent, she was quite adamant about being just fine even though it was pretty evident she needed help. I bet she would have been all right if we hadn't discovered them. Somehow, she'd have found them shelter and enough food to survive on.

"She touched me. Like no female ever has before. I can't explain it very well, but I have strong feelings for her, too. Very strong." He stopped then and let that sink in. Both for himself and for Zane.

In a very soft voice, Zane asked, "Can I please say something now?"

"Sure, knock yourself out. I just don't want to hear anything about you leaving or having doubts about how I feel." Cole reached up with his free hand and pushed a strand of hair off Zane's face.

"Wouldn't dream of it." Zane smiled and pursed his lips, blowing a kiss. "When I saw you and Shira last night, it wasn't just fear that kept me from leaving the cave."

Cole lifted an eyebrow. "No? Then what?"

"She's incredibly attractive, for a female."

"Yes, she is. Curves in all the right places. Nice wide hips, perfect for giving birth."

Chuckling, Zane went on. "That's not exactly what I meant, but that, too." He looked away, gazing towards the stream. "She's more than a good breeder, she's sexy as hell. When I saw you together, it turned me on tremendously. I very nearly joined you."

Cole's mouth dropped open. He'd never dreamed Zane was attracted to her.

Zane continued, "I'd actually wondered what it would be like to share a female. You and I and Shira. But I thought you didn't like them — females. I mean, I knew you'd fucked them in wolf form, but, well… I just didn't know you'd want a female in human form. I guess I figured you'd decided to take a breeding mate, and I was out."

Cole managed to get his mouth closed but not to speak for several moments. *How could we both have been so wrong?* "And I can't believe I thought I'd lost you. I saw you, just for a second, standing at the door. I was afraid you'd think I favoured her. I left this morning because I wasn't ready to face you."

Zane snuggled in closer. "We're in pretty pathetic shape, aren't we?"

"Yeah."

They lay quietly for a few moments, each lost in their own private thoughts. Cole was overjoyed at how Zane felt. He pulled Zane around so they were facing each other. Leaning closer, their lips and noses touching, he whispered, "No matter what else happens, I love you. Remember that, always."

A smile brightened Zane's handsome face. He lifted his head just enough to kiss the tip of Cole's nose.

"I can't believe we both fell for her." Cole chuckled.

Zane smiled and replied in a mock stern voice, "Why not, we both have excellent taste."

It took a second for what he'd said to sink in, then Cole roared with laughter. Zane joined him, and a moment later, they were rolling around their small patch of grass, hugging and tickling each other.

"Hey, what about the talisman?" Cole rolled them both close to the stream and turned to face the running water. Lying on his belly, he reached out and flicked at the water with his thumb and index finger.

"Where is it?" Zane slid his hand over Cole's back, making him shiver with pleasure.

"It's safe among my belongings in the den. I couldn't bear to bring it."

"I know this is your decision, but…"

"What?" Cole asked and looked at him.

Returning his gaze, Zane replied, "The talisman may have already made that choice. It grew warm in your hand. Not in mine, and I'll wager it won't in anyone else's. You need to present it to the clan."

"I know, and I'm truly beginning to believe it belongs to me. I hate the thought of not being free anymore, but perhaps it's time."

"Only 'perhaps'?" Zane asked, obviously wanting Cole to make a firm choice.

Cole squirmed. His life had been good, he balked at letting those freedoms go. But when he thought about it, they were already gone. He loved Zane, and in some strange way he was sure he loved Shira, too.

"Bugger. You just don't let up, do you?" He poked Zane's side and smiled when he heard a sharp grunt.

"Nope, never. I'm not the giving up kind."

"Good, don't ever change."

"Don't plan to. So, only 'perhaps'?" he repeated, his smile broadening.

"No. More than 'perhaps'. The talisman is mine unless it indicates it should go to someone else."

"Finally!" Zane cried.

"Oh, fuck off." Cole laughed and pulled the man close. The warmth of his flesh sent a thrill of pleasure through him. "We need to return and face the pack."

"Yes, and we need to find out what Shira thinks of us."

"True, and of those things, I'm not sure which is going to be the most harrowing."

Zane shifted closer to him. "But first, there's something else we need to do." He pressed his lips to Cole's, and both men sighed.

Chapter Five

Pulling his mouth away, Cole fought to keep from smiling and said in a stern voice, "So, you were spying on me last night. Sneaking around, checking up on who I'm with and what I'm doing."

Zane's face flushed with desire. "Well, uh, I guess I was. I'm sorry, Cole."

"And you think 'sorry' is enough?"

"Probably not. I have a feeling you've got something in mind." Zane leaned forward and kissed him.

Cole thoroughly enjoyed the sensation of their lips sliding together. He fell into the kiss, revelling in the softness of Zane's mouth, the slick wetness of his tongue sliding across his. The world around them seemed to vanish. When he pulled away, it took a moment for him to gather his thoughts. With his heart pounding as if he'd run ten miles, he said, "You think a kiss will lessen your punishment?"

Zane blinked and, for a moment, looked confused. Then he smiled and replied, "I guess I'm pretty transparent, huh?"

"Yes, pretty much."

"Punishment, you said. What kind of punishment could you possibly have in mind?" Zane wriggled his bum.

Cole glanced down at Zane's midsection. An erection pointed up at him. "And that's not going to help you, either." Cole chuckled and pushed himself up onto his feet. Looking around, he spotted a boulder covered with moss. Grabbing Zane by the hand, he pulled the man up and strode over to the rock. "Hands on the boulder, face the stream."

Zane almost fell over his feet in his rush to get into the desired position, while Cole bit his tongue to keep from laughing out loud. With his hands firmly planted on the top of the waist-high boulder, Zane peered back over his shoulder, as if for approval. Cole stepped up closer and placed his hand on the small of his lover's back. Sliding his palm over the firm, warm buttock closest to him, he growled with pleasure. "Not quite right," he said, pushing his foot between Zane's and kicking them apart.

"Hey," the blond man said, stumbling. Only his grip on the rock kept him from falling. He apparently got the message and spread his feet wide apart, offering Cole an amazing view of his bottom as well as access to anything else he wanted.

"Better. Now, arch your back. Show me that beautiful arse."

While Zane obliged, thrusting his bum high into the air, Cole ran a hand over the man's body. Smooth, warm, the well-tanned flesh a joy to explore—he thought of how he'd have all the time in the world to learn what gave Zane the most pleasure. His other hand went to his own crotch, and he hefted the erection jutting from his groin. Sliding his fingers around the shaft, he tugged at his cock and felt it stiffen to its fullest. The mat of pubic hair at the base tickled his hand as he stroked himself.

He watched his beautiful, fair-haired lover arch his back and push his arse even higher. The way Zane had spread his legs allowed his balls to dangle in full view. Cole slid his hand along the crease of Zane's arse, touching the crinkle nestled so sweetly there. A groan encouraged him to press a finger in then twirl it around.

"Tell me what you want," he urged his lover while toying with the man's anus.

"I've been bad. I spied on you. I deserve to be spanked. Please, Cole, my love, spank me."

"But, is a spanking really punishment, or is it something you enjoy?" Cole's finger delved a little deeper into the man's tight arse, while his other hand slid up and down his own shaft. Excitement soared as he waited for the reply.

"I love it when you spank me," Zane confessed, but quickly added, "but I also want it to hurt. The pain feels amazing. It burns and tingles. When you fuck me afterwards, it's like fucking tenfold."

Cole grabbed the base of Zane's cock and squeezed it tight. The explanation was nearly too much for him to hear, taking him so close to coming, he had to fight to control the urge. Just envisioning what was about to happen was driving him nuts.

"So, you misbehave and then you want me to give you pleasure?"

"Yes…uh, no. I mean…" Zane stammered. Apparently, he hadn't thought that far ahead.

"And now you're not even sure what you're asking." Cole found he loved this teasing torment more than he'd thought he would. From Zane's squirming, and the way his erection throbbed in Cole's hand, the man was enjoying it at least as much.

"I want to feel you spank me. I want you to show me that you can control me, punish me when I need it," he murmured.

"Ah, I see." Cole slid his finger into Zane's arse to the hilt. He held it there, wiggling it slightly. The feel of the membrane tight around his digit made him tremble. Taking his time, he slowly withdrew and eased in a second finger alongside the first. "I'll have to think about this. Perhaps you should tell me how much you like it when I fuck you. I know you enjoy talking."

"Yes, oh fuck," the man gasped and shifted his feet even wider apart. "I love how your shaft spreads me wide. It fills me completely. You know just when to speed up, when to stop, when to tease me. I love to feel your cock throb when you come. I can't get enough of it."

"And do you like to suck me off?" Cole asked. He spread the fingers he'd buried in the man's luscious arse, stretching him carefully.

"Yes, yes. Oh, it's so good." Sweat glistened on Zane's back as he chanted his litany of desire.

Another finger slid easily into his lover's clutching hole, and Cole eased all three in and out at a delightfully slow pace. He twisted his wrist and searched for the hard, nutlike prostate gland buried halfway along the man's rectal channel. The slightly different texture told him he'd found it, as did Zane's sudden gasp of sheer bliss when he stroked it and pressed his fingers against it.

His own cock dripped with pre-cum, and he knew he'd need to move the pace along or he'd wind up shooting before he actually got into the warmth of the man's bum. Before that, he had a small chore he wanted to complete.

Releasing Zane's shaft, he ran his palm over the taut rear before him then raised his arm. With his fingers still buried in his lover's arse, he brought his free hand down on the nearest cheek. The man's bum clenched, gripping his digits tight. He lifted his hand again and, as soon as the arse muscles lost their tension, he brought it down hard on the other cheek.

"Ow!" howled Zane, but he didn't move away. The only other reaction was the tightening of his anal muscles.

"You think you can handle a real spanking?" Cole asked, but before the man could reply, he let him have it again as hard as he could, once on each nicely warmed buttock.

A sharp inhalation, followed by a shuddering gasp, and then a gruff, "Yes, sir," was Zane's reply.

"Good." Cole pulled his fingers free and took a step to the side. "Hold still."

"I'll try," Zane whispered. He shifted his feet, preparing himself for what he knew was about to happen.

"Ask me to spank you."

"Damn, you're killing me."

A quick, sharp slap brought another yelp, but also a quick reply, "Please, Cole, spank my arse."

"Again, properly," Cole demanded and raised his hand. He loved how Zane made him feel. He couldn't completely understand why his lover got off on being spanked, but he was more than willing to play along. Another thing they'd explore, he was sure.

"Please, Cole. I've been bad, would you spank me?"

"Yes," Cole replied and brought his hand down, right in the middle of Zane's right buttock. He didn't stop, simply raised his arm and swung again, slapping equally as hard on the left, then again on the right. He alternated between them, adding the occasional swat right between his arse cheeks. After only a few sharp slaps, he noticed the flesh feeling warmer. After a few more, he admired the pleasing shade of bright red.

"Such a sweet arse, so tight and hot," he said and stopped spanking the man to run his palm over the heated cheeks. Handprints showed, blazoned in crimson warmth, the fingertips reaching for hips or thighs.

Cole's cock throbbed, and he ached to replace his fingers with it in the tight entrance and fuck the daylights out of both himself and his lover. Holding off was the most insanely difficult thing he could imagine.

"Please," came Zane's plea, so softly spoken, Cole wasn't sure he'd even heard him.

Moving tighter against his lover's widespread legs, Cole eased his fingers from his anus. "Please, what?" he asked, his own voice deep and husky.

"My cock aches. Touch it again, please." Zane shifted his feet, but otherwise remained as he'd been positioned.

Cole smiled and slid his hand over the well-tanned arse and down along the crease. When he came to the tight pucker, he leaned forward and spat. He rubbed the clear liquid into the man's hole, but didn't linger for more than a few delicious moments. He grasped the dangling ball sac and held him steady while he reached underneath. Zane was hard, and the shaft throbbed when he tightened his fingers around the base.

"Yesss," Zane hissed, and Cole felt him shudder.

"Be still," he growled, sounding much sterner than he felt. He slowly eased his hand forward, drawing the snug flesh of Zane's cock towards the head. He didn't touch the smooth dome. Instead, he pulled his hand back to the man's balls. Cole masturbated him, a few quick strokes alternating with tantalizingly lazy, slow ones, and tried to read his lover's body. When Zane groaned, he stopped and simply held the throbbing shaft for a few moments before continuing with his ministrations. When he was near to bursting himself, he released the cock and balls and eased himself into the man's tight passage.

"Fuck!" He sighed and sank in to the balls. He held himself there, buried to the hilt, his pulse racing, his breath coming in sharp gasps. The pleasure was intense, the need to move almost more than he could stand.

He wanted to drive Zane crazy with lust, though, so he somehow managed to hold off, until he heard a low-pitched, whimpering sound. He pulled back then thrust forward again, slamming his hips into the man's rosy red behind and smiled when the whimper repeated.

"Tell me what you want."

"Fuck me. Damn. Fuck me. Hard." The words blasted out rapid-fire.

Cole raised his hand and brought it down with a resounding slap on Zane's right butt cheek. The left got the same treatment an instant later, then he began to thrust in earnest. Grabbing Zane's hips, he slammed into him with force, only to be answered with cries of pleasure from the fair-haired man.

He felt his balls shift and rise up closer to his body. His head swam as a climax neared. Zane's cries of need and passion were music to his ears. When Zane's arse clenched tight, Cole reached around and again stroked the man's cock. It throbbed in his hand. Like a wild animal bent on escape, it jerked. Pre-cum coated his fingers, smoothing the stroke.

"Now! Oh fuck, now, Cole." Zane pushed his arse back and his muscles tensed. His cock throbbed.

In his mind, Cole imagined a long stream of white cream flying into the air and landing with a splat against the rock.

Cole went wild then, ramming into him while pumping his lover's cock in a rhythm he hoped would send Zane into orbit. He couldn't hold out a moment longer and shoved himself in deep once more. He held himself there, as his world seemed to explode. He roared his bliss and lost sight of everything around him. The forest was gone, the stream faded into nothing. All he knew and cared about was Zane and the pleasure they shared. He shuddered and sent another shot of cum deep into his lover's tight, warm arse.

The gasping and shuddering went on for several minutes. When Cole could catch his breath, he realised his heart was beating like a drum. He gave Zane's cock a final caress before releasing it, then collapsed across his sweat-covered back.

"Thank you," he gasped. He kissed Zane's shoulder and wrapped his arms around the man's body. "I love you."

Zane reached back and stroked Cole's side. "I love you, too. That was amazing."

Chuckling weakly, Cole kissed him again. "Yeah, it was, wasn't it?"

"I think you have to move now. I'm going to collapse."

Cole eased himself out of Zane's bottom but didn't let him go. Helping him to stand up straight, he turned the man so they faced each other. "I want more of that. More of you."

Zane's eyes lit up, and he smiled. "As much and as often as you like."

Cole reached around and gave his bum a gentle slap and chuckled at the grimace.

"Okay, maybe we'll wait a little bit on the next spanking."

"What about something to eat?" Cole looked around, checking for game trails. "I don't know about you, but I'm starving." He spotted a small parting in the brush and footprints.

"I hunt better as a wolf." Zane pulled free of Cole's arms and dropped to his knees.

Cole joined him, and together they shifted. The pain had barely begun before it vanished, changing to the pleasure of becoming the beast. His sense of smell intensified, and his eyesight sharpened, even though the colours faded into a more black-and-white world. He could hear the heartbeat of his lover a few paces away and was overjoyed.

Together they raced for the game path and sniffed. The rich scent of rabbit hung in the air, and Cole's mouth filled with saliva. The trail was fresh, and the rabbit warren was full of plump, wild meat that filled the bellies of the two ravenous beasts.

After their meal, they returned to the stream, and both hunkered forward for a drink of the clear, icy-cold water. The rich taste of blood was quickly washed away, and any spatters of red vanished into the rushing water as they lapped. Thirst quenched, Cole leapt at Zane, and together they raced into the woods.

They spent a good part of the afternoon chasing after each other as they explored the burned out areas. Where there had once been wildlife in abundance, there was now little more than a blackened desert. But, in other places, game flourished, as did the green of the forest. They would pass along the news of where hunting would prove successful and where they'd need to let the greenery return before harvesting could take place.

After another meal of rabbit, they trotted along the slope of a hill. Cole sniffed at Zane's arse and became aroused again. His cock pulsed and emerged from its soft sheath, the tip dripping with pre-cum. He growled low in his throat and nudged his lover's buttock.

'*Horny beast,*' came Zane's eager response to his obvious signal.

'*Yes, horny for you.*'

Zane crouched down with his front end and peered back over his shoulder, his pink tongue flicking across his muzzle. Raising his bottom, he presented Cole with a view of his white, furry arse and the puckered hole just below his tail.

The sex was fast and bestial, with Cole mounting him and entering the dark hole in one lusty shove. Zane pushed back, his anal muscles clenching around Cole's cock, rhythmically tightening then loosening. Cole bit the back of the white wolf's neck, holding to the scruff as he fucked him with abandon. Both males howled as they erupted into a glorious orgasm together.

Later, while they lay by the streamside again, Cole's thoughts returned to the talisman and how his life was changing. When he gazed into Zane's ice blue eyes, he realised how happy he was.

'*Time to return to the pack,*' he sent to his lover

'*Yes, I'm sure everyone is wondering where you are.*'

'*And I need to talk to Shira. She's...*'

'*She's special. I understand that, now.*' Zane leaned forward and slid his muzzle along Cole's neck. '*I love you.*'

'*I love you. Don't ever forget that.*' He rose and headed towards the den.

'*Not a chance.*' Zane sent as he trailed behind.

* * * *

Cole approached the den and paused. He turned and looked at his lover, nuzzling the furry neck he loved to nip. Zane's fur felt warm and sensual. *Damn!* Never before had Cole felt so horny after making love all afternoon. Zane did that to him. Thoughts of Shira excited him as well. The very idea of seeing her again caused his cock to thicken and stretch.

'*Morph?*' Zane's thought wafted over him.

'If we must.' Cole pulled away from his lover and crouched, preparing to return to two-legged form. His bones shifted and elongated, heat and pressure soaring through him. Already aroused, his last coherent thought was that he'd shift into a man with a raging hard-on, and he was right.

When the pain-tinged pleasure subsided, he stood with a fully erect cock next to Zane.

Zane stretched, apparently acclimating to his human stature. He glanced at Cole and grinned. "Look at you. Insatiable."

"That's the fucking truth." Cole stroked his shaft lazily. "I could bend you over right here and easily put it to you again."

Leaning close, Zane blew warm breath on his ear. "Or we could go in and talk to Shira. If everything goes as we hope, we could be sharing her pleasures tonight."

"Yes." Cole nodded, thrusting into his fist one last time. "That sounds good, too."

"Come on." Zane chuckled. He grabbed Cole's hand away from his pulsing erection and tugged him towards the den.

The evening meal appeared to be just over. Several females cleaned eating utensils while the males put away supplies, battening down the exterior of the den for the night. Theron stoked the campfire, while Yive and Meghan attempted to round up the pups and herd them to the river for bathing.

Cole and Zane stepped into the open, catching Shira's attention as she cleaned off tables. She wore a plain garment that barely concealed her curves, which didn't help Cole's erection. There was nothing he could do about it, standing in his full, naked glory before her.

She gazed at them hesitantly, eyes darting from one to the other of them, at their masculinity then away again quickly. She finally spoke when they got closer. "Supper is over. I could fix you something —"

"We've eaten." Cole smiled at her.

She reached up and brushed his face with her thumb. "You caught something, I assume. You've been gone since early morning."

Cole glanced at Zane quickly, then back at her. "We had much to discuss. We'd like to talk to you, if you can spare us some time."

She shrugged. "I've got nothing but time. Your pack has been most kind, but…" Gazing to where the other females and pups gathered and would soon be heading for the river, she murmured, "The others fill their hours with maternal duties. I'm not of this pack, so I'm at a loss for what to do. It's easier for Meghan with the pups."

"Come on." Cole took her arm and led her to the edge of the forest. There were several sawed-off tree stumps there, and he sat on one of them, indicating she and Zane should sit on others.

They followed his lead and looked at him expectantly.

Cole started with an easy topic. "We hoped you and Meghan would feel comfortable with our pack. I know the others would like both you two and the cubs to live with us. It's too quiet without Gar and Ruby. Yive's last litter wasn't healthy, and only the two pups survived."

Zane nodded. "Skip and Hani add a breath of new life to the pack. It's much livelier with four young ones running around."

"Were they of a small litter, too?" Cole inquired. Wolfen litters usually ran between five and ten pups.

Shira nodded. "Some didn't make it. These two were the strongest of the batch." She looked around the woods and inhaled. "I believe Meghan would be happy here. She and her brood fit in well."

"What about you?" Cole asked tentatively.

She gazed into his eyes. "What about me? Last night—" Shira seemed suddenly to remember Zane and broke off her thought with a glance in his direction.

"Go ahead," Cole encouraged. "Zane knows what happened last night. He understands—"

Her eyes blazed, and she slapped her thighs. "How could he, when I don't even understand myself?" She aimed her fury at Cole. "I *thought* we discovered something special with each other. I *assumed* we'd pursue it further today, as we discussed. Then you took off before sunrise and stayed gone all blasted day, with *him*." She tossed a bitter glance in Zane's direction.

"I know, and I'm sorry." Cole folded his arms across his chest. "What happened last night confused the blazes out of me, Shira. I've never had much doubt about my sexuality before. I've always preferred males."

"You've been with females before," she insisted. "You've had to. There's no way you could have made me feel..." She clasped her own arms, looking towards the sky.

Cole saw a shudder pass through her body. He longed to reach out and touch her, but knew that wasn't fair, given the conditions he intended to place on her. He'd made his choice—Zane would be his life-mate. If Shira could live with that, and agreed to join them, he knew they could form a remarkable triad. If she couldn't—wouldn't—consent, then somehow he'd have to find a way to live without her. "Tell me, Shira. How did I make you feel?"

She stared into his eyes. "Like the most cherished, loved female on the planet."

Cole smiled. "Good. That's what I'd hoped for."

She jumped to her feet. "Was it just an act, then? A pretence to get me to spread my legs?"

"Of course not! I was attracted to you, and everything I felt was very real. I wished that to be true for you, as well."

"I've already told you how it was. But you can't imagine how I felt when I woke this morning, and you were both gone."

Here's where the conversation gets tricky. Cole stood and paced in front of her, his erection bobbing as he walked. "I purposely left alone, hoping to avoid both of you. I shifted and ran as far as I could to get away. I needed time to think."

She nodded towards Zane. "He was gone, too."

Cole glanced at him. "He followed me. I'm glad he did. Zane and I needed to talk. We had to figure out our relationship." He turned and faced Shira again. "Before you came along, he and I were casual lovers. It was a semi-regular thing, and it was fucking fantastic, but I was unwilling to commit past one day at a time."

Putting her hands on her hips, she frowned. "So, what? I chased you into his arms?"

"No, it's not like that." Cole sighed. *I'm doing a horrible job of explaining.* "The fire, losing Gar and Ruby…it's been a tempestuous few days. I had some decisions to make. I didn't feel ready before. Today, I do."

"And?" She planted her feet firmly.

Had she been in wolfen form, Cole could envision the hair standing on the back of her neck. *She's a feisty one! I love that about her.* "Shira, I have to be honest with you. I love Zane. My life wouldn't be complete without him as my mate. And he is that, my life-mate."

"Blasted fickle males!" she muttered angrily, stomping about in a circle. She ripped her dress off and tossed it aside.

For a moment, Cole thought she wanted to show him what he'd be missing out on. Her lovely breasts swung heavily as she crouched, and he realised she was preparing to shift.

"Shira, wait! There's more. That's why Zane and I needed to speak with you."

Her voice dripped with sarcasm. "To break the news. Yes, I understand. Thank you for being so upfront. At least I know where I stand." She tossed her head back, and the change began.

Cole watched in amazement as she morphed from the tall, beautiful redhead to a medium-sized she-wolf with a shiny, red pelt. "Damn." He stroked his fully erect cock. "That was hot."

Zane rolled his eyes and stepped next to Cole. "We handled that well." To Shira, he called, "Please don't go. Cole needs to explain his feelings, and he can't seem to do it without getting tongue-tied."

She bared her teeth then turned on her heel and raced into the forest.

"Fuck!" Cole swore, releasing his shaft and once again focusing on the situation at hand.

"Couldn't you just say it?" Zane teased, glancing at him sideways. "The words aren't so hard. *'Shira, I want you, too. We both want you. We want to make love to you right now, all night long.'* That might have done it."

"Fuck yeah, it's easy to say when she's not here! Try saying that, when you're looking into her eyes."

"I could have done it, but it wasn't my place. We'll have to work on this timidity of yours. If you're going to be the leader of the tribe, you'll need to be more forceful. Your words are law, speak them with conviction."

Cole stomped his feet. "I'm not timid! I have no problem speaking my mind. The problem—"

Zane faced him, grinning. "The problem is, when you look into her baby blue eyes, you get all mushy on the inside. And then she flashes those sexy tits, and your cock jumps to attention faster than a rabbit can disappear into a hollow."

"I do *not* get mushy! Shit." Cole looked down, realising Zane spoke the truth. *What kind of leader will I make, falling all over myself at the sight of a woman?*

"Look." Zane placed his hands on Cole's chest and pressed him back against a nearby tree. "It's only because the whole thing is so new. Remember how we used to act? We danced around each other before we were able to admit how we felt and could get down to the serious business of fucking." He placed a kiss on Cole's lips.

"True," Cole murmured then opened his mouth, allowing Zane's tongue entry.

Zane reached for Cole's erection and squeezed it. "Now, things are much easier between us. We know what we want and go for it. You'll get that way with Shira, soon enough. Hopefully, I will, too." His mouth pressed against Cole's as his hand stroked, and he added, "I wouldn't mind getting my hands on those luscious tits. Or tasting what she has to offer between her legs."

"She's a beauty," Cole agreed, picturing her in his mind as Zane worked his shaft. He remembered Shira spreading her legs for him, and how he'd crawled between them. The taste of her sweet nectar was truly magnificent, and the idea of sharing it with Zane sent him over the edge. He gasped and shuddered as streams of creamy, white spunk were coaxed from his cock.

"Oh yeah, oh yeah." Zane murmured repeatedly, their lips still touching. "I love that the thought of the three of us together gets you off that quickly. We're in for some good times, my love."

Cole shook his head, trying to clear it. Zane definitely had the touch. He thought for a moment about reciprocating, but as horny as the two of them were, that might lead to several more hours of play. It sounded nice, but the time wasn't right. *I need to find Shira.*

He gazed into his lover's eyes. "Come with me, help me find her. I need you there."

"Yes, you do," Zane agreed, grinning. He smeared the sticky spunk on their bodies so it would dry and licked his hand. "Mmm."

A rustling in the brush got their attention, and the pup Dib appeared. "They're back!" he called excitedly. "Cole! Kaleb is back!"

"Already?" Cole glanced at Zane. "They made the trip in one day."

"Must have gone straight there and back, stopping just long enough for the burial."

"Unless they couldn't find the bodies." Cole followed Dib through the brush, Zane on his heel.

Inside the cave, Kaleb and Ulric stood by the fire, talking with the other pack members. "Ah, there you are." Kaleb smiled at him.

"Did everything go as planned?" Cole asked.

"Yes." Kaleb nodded. "I was just telling the others, the bodies were exactly where you said they'd be. We took care of them respectfully and spoke a few ceremonial words. Gar and Ruby are in a better place, and I know they're pleased."

Cole watched Kaleb, noting how his mentor spoke clearly and calmly. His voice was firm but soothing to the worried females, especially Tala, Gar's offspring. *Kaleb would make a better tribal leader than I ever could.*

Zane glanced from Kaleb to Ulric. "You made good time."

"It wasn't that long of a trip." Ulric crossed his arms. "When you don't play around half the day."

Cole tried to hold his temper, but Ulric had rubbed him the wrong way that morning and continued in the same vein. "Are you suggesting Zane and I didn't take our trip seriously? I told you we were scouting out the area. We helped a small bear clan tend to their dead and collected items we thought the pack could use."

"Yes, we heard all that." Ulric wiped his hands nervously on the legs of his leather pants. "What we don't understand is why you didn't take care of Gar and Ruby. You keep saying you helped the bears—"

"Ulric, it's done." Kaleb cradled his mate by the back of the neck. "We don't need to speak of them anymore, unless it's to discuss happy memories."

"We need to talk about the talisman," Ulric spouted, and frowned.

"Not tonight." Continuing to speak in an even tone, Kaleb squeezed his shoulders. "We've had a long day. Discussion of the amulet will need to take place, but not now."

"What about the talisman?" Tala stepped forward. "Cole said he never found it."

Ulric snarled. "Then Cole lied."

Zane spoke up. "He never said that. He didn't say anything about the talisman. He didn't want to concern Tala with that when she'd just found out about her father's death." He glared at Ulric. "He was being *tactful*."

"There's no time for tact, now," Ulric snapped back. "We've waited long enough. The wolfen tribe needs a leader. Someone with wisdom and knowledge. Not a man-pup who's biggest concern is racking up the largest number of conquests possible in a day."

"You're being unkind," Yive murmured.

"No, he's being a horse's arse." Zane strode around the fire. "You have the misguided notion the talisman would be better suited to your neck. I contend that no one so judgemental and opinionated should even be in consideration for the role of leader."

"The talisman was my father's," Tala said loudly. "And now it should be mine. Let me hold it, and you'll all see."

"That's absurd!" Ulric muttered, and bickering ensued.

Cole stood back and watched. For some reason, he didn't feel angry anymore. A sense of calmness spread like a blanket over him. The amulet would ultimately disclose itself and make the choice.

Kaleb watched him with an amused smile on his face. Cole gazed at him, trying unsuccessfully to read his mentor's thoughts. He looked back at the pack members, all of them red-faced and flinging angry words at each other.

He turned and went into his sleeping chamber, quickly donning a loincloth and grabbing one for Zane. He retrieved the talisman from the nook in which he'd hidden it. Carrying it carefully in his hand, he returned to the others.

"I have the talisman," he announced, tossing the second loincloth to Zane.

Arguments ceased.

"I want it!" Tala cried.

"Give it to me," Ulric demanded.

Cole dangled the brilliant stone by its leather cord so everyone could see it. "I'm not sure it's mine to give away."

"Cole is right." Kaleb stepped forward. "No one picks the talisman. It's the other way around. The amulet chooses its owner, you all know that." He smiled at Cole. "Hold the gem in your hand, my son."

Shifting it to his palm, Cole held it so all could see. The opalescent stone glowed, casting warm heat in his hand.

Yive and Theron gasped and took a step back. Murmurs of awe came from the pups and some other pack members.

"Yes!" Zane rushed to Cole's side. "The amulet glows for Cole. It did nothing in my hand."

"Show them." Cole passed the stone into his lover's palm.

Zane held it in the same manner, palm up, but the stone remained dark and cool.

"Let me try!" Tala shoved forward, her hand outstretched.

Zane glanced at Cole, and he nodded.

She nearly snatched the leather thong from Zane, but once it was in Tala's possession, the stone appeared unchanged. She squeezed it as if that might bring it to life, but nothing happened.

"Yes." Kaleb nodded. "I should have thought of this before." He took the amulet from Tala and passed it around. Even the pups had the opportunity to hold it, but the stone didn't change.

Kaleb faced his mate, the last person in line to hold the gem. "Ulric, my love. Take the talisman. Understand what it is saying to you."

Shaking, Ulric reached for the leather thong and grasped the stone. He stared so intensely at it, Cole thought the thing might explode from the weight of his gaze. Nothing happened, and Ulric swore, squeezing the talisman. "No!" He dropped to his knees.

Kaleb reached for his mate. "Calm yourself, heart of my heart. This wasn't meant to be. I think we both knew that."

Zane stepped forward. "Give the talisman back to Cole. He is the rightful holder."

Ulric looked up, his face bright red and tear-streaked. "He doesn't deserve it! He hasn't earned it. The boy has no life experience and doesn't even have a mate, for Hades' sake!"

"He deserves it." The female voice came from behind Cole, and all heads turned to see who spoke.

Shira stood there in her simple garment, one hand resting against the stone wall. She glanced around the group and stopped, focusing on Cole. "He's got more wisdom and maturity than you know. And he has a fine mate in Zane. But none of that really matters. The talisman chose him, didn't it?"

Easing the amulet from Ulric's hand, Kaleb passed it to Cole. When he accepted it, the stone warmed, again glowing a deep, brilliant red.

Kaleb smiled. "Shall I place it around your neck, my leader?"

Cole glanced from him, to Zane then to Shira. "Not yet." He clutched the amulet. "There's something I need to do before I can fully accept the responsibility." He strode towards Shira and motioned to Zane. "Come with me."

Chapter Six

"We need to talk." Cole clasped Shira by the arm.

"That's not necessary." She shook her head.

"Of course, it is. I badly fumbled our last conversation. This time, I'm going to get it right." Maintaining his grip on her, he led Shira back into the forest with Zane following. He went farther this time, to a secluded, grassy clearing that was bathed in the light of the setting sun.

"What are we doing?" Shira glanced around.

"Sit." Cole led her to a tree stump and forced her down. He knelt in front of her. "I don't want to take the chance of messing this up again, so I'm just going to say it. I want you, Shira. I have since the moment we met. Our night together only confirmed that fact."

She gazed at him with a shocked expression. "I don't understand. You said you loved Zane."

He took her hand. "I do love Zane, deeper than I ever thought I could love anyone. But what I feel for you can't be denied. Strong, passionate, intense feelings. I can't let them go. We need more time together, of course, but I think…" he paused.

"Go on, just say it," Zane murmured from beside him.

Cole's words spilled out in a rush. "I think I might love you, too."

Shira's face softened. "Oh, Cole. I can't believe you're saying this. I just spent the past hour cursing you in my mind. I guess I jumped to all the wrong conclusions."

"There's a lot of that going around." Zane smiled. "Cole and I had much to talk about today. If we're going to be a triad, we'll all need to be able to speak openly with each other."

She glanced up at him. "A triad? Is that what you're proposing?"

"Yes." Cole squeezed her hand. "When I told Zane we'd been together, he admitted he'd seen us. And wanted to join us. He found our mating very hot."

"Is that so?" Shira pulled her hand away and stood. She walked in front of Zane, and they circled each other. She sniffed at him, as she'd done when they'd first met.

Zane, with an amused smile on his face, allowed her to check him out.

"I've never been part of a triad," she finally said.

Zane raised his eyebrows. "I believe you'll find it very pleasurable." He glanced at her nearly exposed tits. "I know I will."

"Seems like there would be lots of room for jealousy," she countered, still pacing.

"We'd simply have to try hard not to let that happen. Communication is the key."

Shira stopped and cupped her crotch. "I will be Cole's breeding partner. Only his cock will touch me here."

Zane grinned. "There are plenty of other places for my cock to play, if you're interested. The choice, beautiful she-wolf, is yours."

"The choice is Cole's," she insisted. "If Cole is my mate, I bow to his wishes."

Cole stepped next to her. "I've made my choice. I want to make love to you, Shira. Zane and I want to make love to you. We'll do whatever we can to make you happy."

She stared into his eyes, touching her stomach lightly. "I want pups."

He grasped her hips. "I'll give you all the pups you can handle. Our broods will be healthy and strong."

Shira looked at the ground then gazed up at him. "Will we ever have time to be alone together, just you and me?"

"If you desire it. Just as I might want some time alone with Zane. And Zane—who knows what he's going to want or need. But we'll be equal partners, each having a say in the relationship."

"I'm still not sure how it might work," she murmured. "But I'd like to try."

"Woo hoo!" Cole swung her into his arms. "That's what I prayed you'd say. Just try. Time will tell if we've made the right choice."

"I think so, too." She nodded then shimmied from his grasp and faced Zane. She reached out and tugged at his loincloth. "I want a more thorough inspection of you."

He smiled. "I walk around naked half the time. You've seen me."

"Not like this." She wrapped her fingers around his shaft and brought it to erection. "Not where I could examine you fully. Taste you. Explore every inch of you."

Eyeing her levelly, he thrust into her hand. "I intend to do the same."

"Then let's get started." Shira dropped to her knees, drawing Zane's cock into her mouth.

"All right, then." He inhaled as she sucked firmly. His legs wobbled, and he reached out, looking for balance.

"Lean against me, my beautiful man." Cole approached him from behind, drawing the long, white hair aside and kissing his neck.

"Always." Zane turned his face sideways, and they kissed, tongues delving deep.

Cole swallowed Zane's groans as Shira devoured the man. He felt the shudders of his lover's body as she worked him over aggressively. He could tell by Zane's ragged breathing that his orgasm was imminent. "That's it," he coaxed. "Spill it. Let her taste what you have to offer. Later, I'm going to want to taste you."

Zane grinned and moaned. "Close. So close."

"Let me breathe for you." Cole attached his mouth to his lover's and held on tight. He felt when Zane released. His man shook and shimmied, tried desperately to remain standing. Cole held him tight, vowing never to let him fall.

Shira's groans of approval were equally arousing. Cole watched her coax the last drops of cum from Zane's shaft then sit back on her haunches. "You have a pleasing cock," she announced.

Zane and Cole burst into laughter. "Well, thanks."

Cole wasn't sure he'd ever seen the man's face flushed so brightly pink. He smiled. "I think you have a very pleasing cock, too. I guess I just never told you."

"No, you haven't. But thanks. So, is it my turn to choose what will please me?"

"Absolutely." Cole stepped back, already knowing what his stud was after.

Zane dropped to his knees in front of Shira. "You, lying on your back, with my face between your legs. That's what I've been fantasising about."

She couldn't scramble away quickly enough. Shira lifted her arms and tore her dress off, tossing it aside.

"Oh, yeah." Zane eased her onto the soft grass and held his body mere inches above hers. He played over her skin, never quite touching it with his lips, as he moved from her face to her breasts.

Shira groaned, his torment obviously arousing her. She thrust her chest forward, offering a breast to his mouth.

"Beautiful," Zane murmured, before grazing the nipple with his teeth.

"More," she groaned.

He covered the brown nubbin with his mouth, sucking the bud Cole knew was so tasty.

Unable to resist, Cole dropped to her other side and drew that nipple into his mouth. She tasted of sweat and woman, a delicious mix.

Zane grinned at him over their shared feast and maintained the suction on her tit. His hands roamed over her flat stomach, while Cole's hands roamed over Zane.

Shira's hips bucked up and down. "More, please!"

"Such a greedy girl." Zane squeezed the flesh of the tit he worshipped. "I could suckle here all day, if I didn't know what awaited me."

"Moving on, then?" Cole tweaked Zane's flat nipple as his mouth pressed against Shira's fleshy mound.

"I suppose. Care to join me?"

"I'll be right behind you."

Zane grinned. "I love it when you're behind me." He slipped between Shira's thighs and pushed them apart, examining her intimately. "So lovely. When I saw Cole's face here, so many emotions went through me. First, I wanted to be Cole. Then, I wanted to be next to him, enjoying you as a pair."

"Show me." Shira jiggled her legs open and closed.

Cole peered over Zane's shoulder as his fair-haired lover spread the pink pussy lips. Zane flicked his tongue over her clitoris, and they both watched her jump.

"That's so fucking hot," Cole murmured, running his hands over Zane's muscular back.

"Slip in here and join me," Zane offered. "I'll share with you, and steal some musky flavoured kisses at the same time."

"That sounds intriguing, to be sure." Cole moved behind Zane. "But I have something else in mind. Don't worry about me." He spread Zane's arse cheeks and admired the puckered hole between them. "Ah, yes." Cole drove forward, spearing the anus with his tongue.

"Sweet mercy!" Zane gasped. "You'll have me hard again in no time."

Cole wedged his nose between his buttocks and grinned. "I intend to keep you hard, my gorgeous stud. You never know when I, or this luscious female, might need attention." His words were intended to tease, but the very idea made Cole's cock harden and weep. He smeared the tip of his shaft on one finger and inserted it into Zane's tight channel.

His handsome lover groaned, his words breathy. "At your service, my leader. Anytime, day or night. And as for this tasty morsel..." He dived into Shira's pussy face first, lapping her juices with ardour.

"Yes!" Shira cried out. "Take me! Take me now."

Cole leaned up to watch her climax. He licked his lips as Zane speared the moist pussy with three fingers. The simulated fuck apparently drove her over the edge, and she moaned and panted as her body quivered.

Zane flicked her clit until the shudders subsided then slowly laved her folds with long, wet strokes.

Cole grasped his cock. He was rock hard and near bursting. "I can't bear to watch this anymore."

"Don't just watch." Zane rolled off to the side, moving over Shira's leg. He clasped one hand around Cole's shaft and guided it to the fully lubricated pussy. "She wants to be taken. Do it! Take her now, and let me savour it."

"Fuck!" The most pleasant sensations were running through Cole's body. To feel Zane's hands on him, then Shira's, was intense and more wonderful than he could have imagined. He sank into her pussy, his cock claiming the territory it desired.

"Oh, yeah." Zane began stroking himself. "Fuck her. Grind it out. I really want to watch you come."

Shira looked at him. "You said it yourself—don't just watch." She gazed up at Cole. "Remember the neat trick from before?"

Cole grinned. He absolutely remembered. "Of course. Do you want that?"

"Please." She clung to his shoulders as Cole gripped her arse and flipped them over.

Shira sat astride him, his cock firmly planted inside her. She straightened, tossing her hair over one shoulder. "Zane." She gazed at him. "Come, join us. Fuck me at the same time our lover does."

Zane's eyes lit up. "Have you ever…"

"No." Shira ran a hand over her smooth arse. "You can be my first."

Zane straddled Cole's legs, sitting close behind her. "You'll be tight. It might be uncomfortable."

She smiled over her shoulder at him. "I'm sure you can handle tight. And as for comfort, well, I tried to get Cole to fuck me like an animal today, but he disappeared. Perhaps you can be the one to do it."

Cole saw Zane's mouth twitch, as if it were watering. He grinned up at him. "Go ahead, lover. Shira wants it a little rough. Think you can handle that?"

"Oh, I think so." Zane moved behind her, but the last expression Cole saw looked as if the man had died and gone to heaven.

Cole held still, not wanting to resume thrusting and risk coming too soon. He'd give Zane a chance to catch up. "She'll need to be stretched and lubricated," he reminded him.

"I've got it," Zane replied. "I'm dripping lubrication. And the stretching will be my pleasure. How does that feel, Shira? That's one finger."

"Oh, yes." A look of blissful disbelief crossed her face.

"I think she likes it, my love." Cole reached up and tweaked one of her deep brown nipples.

"Then let's try two."

Cole wished he could see Zane penetrating Shira's virgin arse. Next time, he'd be where he could watch and stroke himself. But now, her pussy felt warm and wet, wrapped around his shaft like a glove. He couldn't be stuck in a better spot.

"Ah, nice and pliant." Zane groaned from behind. "Three fingers, my sexy she-wolf. Your outer ring has relented. Soon, my cock will slide right in."

"If you keep talking, I'm going to shoot right now." Cole closed his eyes, trying to hold back his orgasm.

Shira rose up and down on him teasingly.

"Stop! Stop!" He shook his head. *Close. So fucking close.*

"It feels so good, Zane," she murmured. "Please, take me now. Fuck me with your beautiful cock. See if you can feel Cole's shaft rubbing against you."

"Shit." Zane repositioned himself.

Cole could feel every move he made. The tip of his bulky rod slipped into her arse an inch, and Zane pressed for more.

"So tight," Zane muttered through gritted teeth.

"Yes, fuck me!" Shira commanded as her body accepted the intruder.

Cole felt the long shaft through her thin membrane wall and couldn't hold back any longer. He resumed his thrusts, as hard as he was able to with two bodies above him. The weight and pressure made it that much more intense.

"Oh, fuck!" Zane called. "I'm not going to last long."

"Come with me." Cole felt his balls lift. His climax was right there. One more nudge, and he'd fly over the edge.

Shira wailed, and his eyes flew open. For a moment, he worried they were hurting her, but the expression on her face indicated anything but pain. She panted and gasped, her pelvic muscles contracting around his shaft.

Cole erupted. His seed shot out in spurts, again and again. It was all he could do to remain conscious. When he finally opened his eyes, he saw those of both his lovers closed. Zane's arms were wrapped around Shira's torso tightly, a hand cupping one of her full breasts.

He mustered the energy to speak. "That was incredible."

Zane kissed Shira's neck, and she turned her head to accept another directly on the mouth. They kissed for long moments, and Cole's heart soared. He no longer had doubts. This was right, he felt it. Zane and Shira were his chosen mates. They would love passionately, make an abundance of pups and gently rule the wolfen tribe with their mixture of hearts, minds and souls.

"Be still while I pull out," Zane told Shira. "Your body has contracted around mine. This might hurt a bit."

"Then never pull out." Shira reached for his face and another kiss.

Cole snickered. "I might need the use of my legs again sometime."

"Tough." Zane grinned at him then clutched Shira's hips. He backed away carefully.

She groaned, then pressed Cole's abdomen to release his staff. Rolling to his side, she nuzzled into the crook of his arm. "By the gods," she murmured.

"Incredible," Cole repeated.

Shira glanced up at Zane, who rested on his haunches. "Come lie with us, my new lover. I need a few moments, but I haven't had my fill of you, yet."

Zane smiled, moving towards them.

"Wait." Cole glanced at him. "Do something for me?"

"Anything, you gorgeous hunk."

Cole motioned to the side. "Under my loincloth. Could you bring it to me?"

Zane stood and walked to where they'd shed their clothing. He raised Cole's loincloth and they all spotted the talisman. His eyes lit up. "Are you sure?"

"I'm sure. If you two are willing to undertake this journey with me."

Zane picked up the amulet and returned to them. "There's no question how I feel. I'd love nothing more than to stand by your side." He grinned. "Or behind you, or bent in front of you—wherever you'll allow me to stand."

Cole chuckled. "All of the above, anytime you like. But seriously, this is a huge responsibility. I can't do it alone."

Zane knelt and both men looked at Shira.

She smiled. "I don't think you'll be doing anything alone for quite some time." She stroked Cole's cheek. "I, too, accept your offer and the obligations that come with it. Happily."

Cole sat up, bringing her with him. He looked at Zane. "Would you do the honours?"

Zane offered one end of the talisman's leather thong to Shira. "Shall we do it together?"

She nodded and took the strap. Together they tied it around Cole's neck, and each left one hand on his shoulder.

The sparkling, red stone glowed brighter than Cole had ever seen it.

"Look at that!" Shira marvelled.

"This was truly meant to be." Zane's eyes twinkled.

Cole reached for both his mates and drew them into an embrace. "But then, we knew that, didn't we?"

Epilogue

Cole glanced out over the green fields of the wolfen territory. It had been an abundant spring with plentiful rain, and evidence of the fire was getting harder to find. "The land looks good," he remarked, pleased.

"The wildlife is returning, as well." Kaleb grasped a handful of bulrush roots. "When I was out hunting this morning, I saw several families of rabbits and deer in the new growth. I was in such a good mood, I couldn't bear to pursue any of them. So we'll have roots and berries one more night." He shrugged.

Laughing, Cole shook his head. "You old softie. I'll send Ulric with you tomorrow. He won't mind hunting prey for a good meal."

"You're right." Kaleb chuckled. "He keeps me in line. So, what have you got there?" He peered around Cole, trying to see what he held behind his back.

"Nothing." Cole stepped sideways so Kaleb couldn't see.

"What is it?" Kaleb wrestled him jovially.

Cole gave in, showing a handful of wildflowers.

"Aw, those are sweet." Kaleb nudged him.

"Shut up." Cole muttered, feeling the heat of a flush rise to his face.

"You have to admit, a male mate doesn't require as much special treatment. Between you and Zane, with his treks to find Shira's favourite berries, she keeps you two hopping."

"We only do what we wish to do," Cole insisted.

"I'm sure." Kaleb continued to tease. "It's your wish to spend long hours rubbing her back and feet."

"It is." He rolled his eyes and turned back towards the den. "She's earned it. The pups will birth any day now, and by the size of her belly, there'll be a bunch of them."

Kaleb grabbed the scruff of Cole's neck as they walked home. "And my boy will be a father. Honestly, I never thought I'd see the day. Especially when you met Zane. I figured he'd be the one you settled down with."

"Zane and I are very happy." Cole shrugged off his grasp. "Shira completes us, and makes us happier. It's the perfect arrangement."

"For you, I believe it is. I'm proud of you, Cole."

"Thanks, Kaleb. Your support means everything in the world to me."

"You'll always have it."

They stopped when they reached the edge of the compound. Zane approached from another direction, a bowl full of ripe, red berries in his hand.

"You're so whipped." Kaleb shook his head, grinning.

"Ignore him." Cole slid his arm around his mate's waist. "He's jealous that Shira's reached the horny part of pregnancy." He glanced back at Kaleb and winked. "She says multiple orgasms each day will make the delivery easier. We're lucky there are two of us. One man might lose a tongue trying to keep up with that she-wolf."

"We do what we must." Kaleb nodded wisely, heading off to his own alcove.

"Shall we go check on her?" Cole turned back to Zane.

"In just a minute." He pulled Cole's face to his for a slow, deep kiss. "I'll never get enough of you. After we've seen to Shira's needs, I want you to fuck me. It's been too long."

"It hasn't been a full day!" Cole protested laughingly.

"That's far too long. Trust me."

The talisman glowed dimly around Cole's neck, a feeling he'd grown used to over time. It had varying degrees of heat, signalling different things to take note of, and validating Cole's thoughts and emotions. When it indicated happiness, pure and complete satisfaction, the heat level was at its most pleasurable. And that one never went away.

STALLION'S PRIDE

Dedication

To Kai, Aric and Sable, Tarek, Raven and Inuku, Cole, Zane and Shira, Brishen, Jal and Tawnie. Thank you all for an amazing ride.

Chapter One

Brishen's thoughts raced. The cool evening air had his flesh crawling with goose bumps, his nipples erect. Tawnie, her supple body tanned and eager, pressed against him. Yet, the moonlight and her presence couldn't distract him from where his mind continued to wander. His father, Shandor, lay abed, ill for some months with age and a hacking cough that wouldn't let him rest. Pesha, his mother, tended the old man, easing his discomfort, but there was little else she could do. Shandor's life had been long and filled with troubles, as had the lives of all of their *vitsa*, or clan. Years of mistrust and battle with other *vitsas* had taken its toll on them all. Mares lost foals too often, and many of the young stallions fought amongst themselves, even within *familya* groups.

"Brishen, don't be so stubborn," Tawnie murmured, her arms reaching around his neck, her body pressing ever closer to his. Her lips, ripe and succulent looking, pursed for a kiss as she rose onto her toes and leaned in.

Brishen straightened, peering over the top of the lovely woman's head. The tree lined valley with the meandering river running through its centre was ideal for the families. The field of rich grasses and clover fed their equine form. There were pockets of shrubbery where berry and wild apple trees grew in abundance. Some homesteader must have abandoned the area years ago, he thought, trying to push the vision of his wasted father from his mind.

"Hey." Tawnie grabbed his ears and dragged his face down so she could see into his eyes. "I'm still here, remember me?" Her voice was soft, but her deep brown eyes shone with a brightness that surprised him.

"Yes, I know you are, and I could never forget you." He smiled, a little weakly he knew, but he hoped it reassured her. After all, she was the woman chosen for him by his father. He reached around her, resting his hands on her wide, muscular hips. A granite boulder behind him was at just the right height for him to perch his arse on. He drew her with him as he shifted, the thread-bare jeans not doing anything to cushion his bottom.

The woman smiled, her wide eyes appearing even brighter in the moonlight. "Yeah, I know, you've got a lot on your mind right now. I just thought I might be able to distract you for a while." She swivelled her hips, grinding herself against his slowly rising cock.

"The wars between our *vitsas* are killing us," he mused. "We need to find a way to live in peace with the others before there are too few of us to keep the *natsia* of horse changelings alive." He gazed into her eyes then leant forward, pressing his lips to hers in a desperate effort to forget his woes, if only for a short time. Even as his lips parted and his tongue delved into the sweetness of her mouth, he found his thoughts going to another.

Jal, his friend for as many years as he could remember, troubled his mind. Tall, even taller than himself, Jal was black skinned and insanely handsome.

He tore his lips from Tawnie's and turned his face to the side. Confused and feeling more alone than ever before, he wanted to cry out his frustration but dared not. How could he let anyone know how he felt about his friend?

"I understand the burdens you bear. But what troubles you so, right now, my love?" Tawnie stroked his shoulder and arm.

Her touch was like silk, the tips of her fingers sending a shiver down his spine. Closing his eyes, he wondered what to say. *What will placate her without causing her any more discomfort? Best to stick with the concerns I have for my father.*

When he opened his eyes again, the night had darkened, yet still her eyes sparkled when he found them with his gaze. "My father troubles me, his illness, his weakness. I wonder how much longer he has to live. What will become of our *familiya* when he passes? Or, for that matter, the whole gypsy *natsia*?"

Frowning, Tawnie remained silent for a moment. "He's still strong. He'll pull through," she said.

Brishen pushed himself up off the boulder and away from her embrace. He walked towards the river, his boots sinking into the loam. Others shared Tawnie's delusions, but he knew the truth. His father wasn't strong anymore. Shandor hadn't been able to keep the various *vitsas* from fighting for a long time. He'd become the king in name only, and the gypsy nation suffered because of it.

He heard her stumbling after him, her footfalls light but discernable.

"Brishen, where are you going?" She sounded annoyed.

He couldn't blame her. He'd been dodging her for weeks, ever since his father had decided she was an acceptable mate for him.

He spun and faced her. She was only a few steps from him and stopped when her breasts came near to touching his naked chest. He glanced down at the lovely mounds stretching the soft cotton of her blouse and smiled. "Maybe I just wanted to see you approach me."

Tawnie's jaw sagged open. Her eyes bulged. "Wha..."

Tension broken, Brishen laughed.

When, a moment later, she closed her mouth and raised her open hand as if to slap him, he laughed even harder. Compared to her, he was huge. Men of his family were always much larger than the women, and he towered over most.

"Bastard," she growled, then she, too, chuckled. "Yes, you are a bastard, but a handsome one." Tawnie slipped her hands under his forearms and raised them, until he automatically wound them around her upper body and pulled her into another embrace. Her face lay against his chest, and she spoke just loud enough for him to hear. "I would share your burden if you'd let me."

He pressed his lips into the soft waves of her nearly white hair, kissing them. She felt good in his arms, and his erection grew again, pressing against his jeans. She must have felt the bulge, because the next thing he knew, her hips were swaying side to side and her hands had him by the arse.

Brishen slipped his palms down her back to where her blouse lay against the top of her skirt. He slipped his fingers under the hem and grabbed then lifted it, baring her smooth skin.

"Yes, oh yes, Brishen," she murmured against his chest. She lifted her arms, allowing him to slip the blouse off her and toss it onto the grass. Her skirt was easy. The elastic waistband took only a second to push down over her hips. Let go, it fell to the grass at her feet.

Her fingers busily worked at his fly, pushing it down. He kicked off his boots and let her shove off his jeans. Naked, they entered each other's arms again, his erection trapped between them. It pulsed against her belly. He found himself concentrating on the sensation of her soft skin sliding every so sweetly across his glans.

Tearing his mind from his own pleasure, he stepped back and laid his hands on Tawnie's shoulders. While looking deeply into her eyes, he slipped his fingers towards her dark nipples, the tips distended and reaching for him. The crinkled nubbins stood proud like tiny beacons atop the generous mounds of her breasts. When his finger brushed one, Tawnie moaned and thrust her chest out, apparently wanting more of whatever he was giving.

Brishen tweaked the tip, turning and tugging at the delicate tissue until her soft moan turned into a sobbing cry of need. Beads of sweat trickled towards the cleft separating each abundant mound, and he leant down to lick at the salty nectar. His dick moved, thrusting itself harder against her. He shoved his hips forward again and gritted his teeth to keep from groaning.

"You're driving me crazy, woman," he whispered huskily. He leant forward, his hips pulled away from her, leaving his cock jutting out between his thighs. He tongued her free nipple then gently bit at the taut flesh.

"Good, I like you crazy," she murmured into his ear. She slid her hands along his shoulders, massaging the muscles.

Brishen reached down between her thighs until the warm dampness of her sex brushed the back of his hand. The pubic hair tickled, and he pressed upwards. Too soft, he mused. For an instant, he craved the hard body of a man. Not any man, but Jal.

He shook himself, driving the thought away, and returned to gently rubbing the delicate folds of her pussy. Her body moved with him, swaying backwards and forwards.

"Hey, Brishen," came the deep, masculine call of the man he'd been fantasising about moments before. "Brishen! It's your father. He needs you."

Brishen pulled away from his lovely partner and peered in the direction of Jal's voice. The tall, ebony skinned man raced towards them, his unfastened shirt flapping behind him. A tight pair of jeans hugged the man's muscular thighs, and his boots thudded into the loam as he approached them.

Brishen reached for his own rough jeans and quickly slipped them on. Beside him, Tawnie slid into her skirt and was just pulling her blouse on over her head when Jal came to a halt a few paces away.

"Your father called for you." Jal's dark brow creased with concern. His voice quavered. "Pesha looks like she's been crying. You'd better hurry."

Even in the growing dark, Brishen saw Jal bite back whatever he'd been about to add. The man's jaw clenched, and he shifted from foot to foot as if eager to be on his way.

Gut-clenching fear for his father tightened Brishen's stomach. "Will you see that Tawnie gets back all right?" He gave the woman a quick peck on the nose before moving in the direction of his family's dwelling.

"Yes, she'll be fine. Now go," Jal said urgently.

After a dozen paces, Brishen began his change. Legs lengthened, and his arms grew heavy. His neck thickened, and he leant forward to balance the weight. Hooves formed, and his fingers and toes burned for the merest second at the transformation. Muscles bulged in his rump as his body elongated. The wind pulled at his emerging mane, and his face ached for the seconds it took to become the muzzle of his horse shape. The remains of his clothing and boots fell away in his haste for speed.

Over his shoulder, Brishen saw Jal take the woman's arm. Relieved, he took off at a gallop.

* * * *

Brishen stopped only when he'd reached his father's wagon and again took on the guise of a man, grunting at the quick transformation. Naked, he climbed the steps at the rear of the structure and tapped on the wooden frame. Not waiting for an answer, he drew the curtain away and stepped inside.

A robe hung beside the door, and he quickly donned it. Crates and boxes were stacked high along the back part of the dwelling. The front was taken up by his parents' bed, now piled with blankets covering the shrivelled body of his father. His mother, a small, wiry, white-haired woman who had more strength than many men of the *vitsa*, sat on a low stool beside the bed, his father's hand in hers.

She faced Brishen, tears trickling down her cheeks. "Shandor called for you. Thank the stars you got back in time." She glanced at her man then back at Brishen, her eyes shadowed with sorrow. "He's weak, very weak." Pesha got up and stretched, her dull, cotton dress billowing around her slender body. "Come, you sit. I need to move around for a few minutes." She reached out and laid her palm against Brishen's chest and said, "Be strong, my son, and listen well to your father." Pesha ducked out, a sigh following her into the night.

"Brishen," came the all too familiar wheeze of his father's voice. "Is that you, my son?"

Brishen turned, went to his father's bedside and sat on the stool his mother had just vacated. The smell of illness surrounded him, and a great sadness tore at his heart. "Yes, father, it's me." Leaning forward, he took his father's gnarled hand in his and squeezed it carefully.

"Good," the old man said and turned towards him. The face bore more lines than a creek bed in summer when the soil dried and cracked. Yet, there still remained laugh lines around the eyes that made Brishen's heart ache. It had been much too long since the man had laughed.

"What can I do to aid you, my father?"

"It's time to move my bed. Set up a canopy in front of the wagon."

"Father, no." Brishen knew his father believed in the custom that a gypsy must not die in his own home. The death bed needed to be moved to a public place where the tears and lamentations of his *familya* could be publicly displayed.

"It is time, my son. But first, I need to tell you something. I had a dream." Shandor sank back into the cushions. "A very strange dream I want to share with you. It has meaning, I'm sure of it."

Settling against one of the wooden crates, Brishen smiled. "A dream with meaning. Tell me, I could use some distraction." *Distraction indeed,* he thought and remembered Jal's naked chest heaving when he'd arrived at the clearing where Brishen had been with Tawnie. The man excited him, and he couldn't escape it. *Not sure I want to.*

The old man's words dragged him back, and he listened.

"You know how I feel about the constant fighting among our *vitsas*. We cannot seem to agree on anything, and our entire *natsia*, our nation, suffers for it. I fear for your future once I'm gone. The fighting is bound to grow worse."

"Yes, and you know I agree and understand your concern." Brishen laid his hand on his father's arm, hoping to give comfort through his touch. "What does this have to do with your dream?"

A wracking cough kept Shandor from replying immediately.

Brishen helped the man sit up then gave him a sip of water.

When he was able, his father went on. "Many years ago, there was a man, or more precisely a changeling, named Cato. He was unlike us in many ways, but alike in others. His *natsia* or tribe were cats, cougars from the mountains.

"In my dream, it was like I was this Cato. His people had troubles just like ours, fighting, the young killing each other over nothing. One day, he and his mate, Kissa, found some things that changed their lives, ended the conflicts — theirs and those of other changeling *natsias* — wolves and bears. They found amulets, one for each of the different *natsias*. The amulets had mystical stones that gave the holders great power."

"Power?" Brishen perked up, wondering what power an amulet could give its wearer and why this was all so important now.

"Yes, power to bring the *vitsas* together, to bring peace to the *natsias*." Shandor seemed stronger, his voice determined to get his entire message across. "Each amulet had a different coloured stone, and one of the gems spoke to Cato, chose him as the first holder. It told him of a way for all the *vitsas* to live in peace. Each stone had to be given to the race indicated by the delicate threads of gold shaped into the form of the species. Among those *natsias*, only one could hold the talisman. That one must have a life mate who would stand with him through everything. He must also have the good of his entire breed in his heart.

"It was an enormous task, but one Cato and Kissa gladly took on. First, they travelled between the cougar clans, going from one to the next, covering all the territory where they knew their kind flourished. The amulet gave them the power to show the *familiyas* that if the fighting continued, the changelings would soon die. They succeeded not only by explaining verbally but by reaching into the very minds of their fellow cats. Some protested, but many more wanted peace and quickly hushed their angry cries. Mothers, grandmothers, fathers and the young, all craved harmony between the cougar *vitsas*. The young men, those who sought glory or to show their bravery, were the ones who craved battle. In vivid, gory detail, Cato showed them the error of their ways in a manner that only true mind-to-mind communication could do. He showed them that if they continued to kill each other while other clans also sought power, in only a few generations the *vitsas* would all die out. There was no way to contest the visions." Another bout of torturous hacking stopped Shandor from going on for long moments.

Brishen helped his father sit up again and held him tightly while the wracking cough took its course. *How long can this last?* His father's words confused yet excited him, and he knew he had a great deal to think about.

"Father, you still haven't told me what this has to do with our *natsia*. We were never contacted, never had anything like this amulet you speak of," Brishen said in a soft voice.

Lying back, his eyes closed, Shandor went on. "That is true, my son, but let me finish the story.

"To end the conflict, each *vitsa* had to swear allegiance to the holder of the amulet. When he was sure the cougar *natsia* was going to survive, Cato and his mate moved on to the other changelings — the bears and the wolves.

"It took them many months to complete their task. The amulets showed him who was to become their holder, warming the palm of the right man when held. It did nothing if the wrong one took it up. Only those the amulet deemed worthy could keep the charm, and only those who were mated for life could keep it for long.

"This Cato was the father of all changeling leaders. There was peace for many generations, the talismans going to new owners when the old passed on." Shandor sighed and shifted against the bedding.

"Like a king." Brishen shrugged. Gypsys had been ruled by kings and queens as far back as history recalled. *Doesn't seem so unusual.*

"Not every *natsia* has kings, my son. Some consider that the old fashioned way."

Brishen nodded. For a moment, he thought the old man was done talking and wondered, again, what all this had to do with them. He settled his back against the crate and thought of Jal. What would his handsome friend think of his father's story? What would the others think?

In a voice grown weak from the storytelling, Shandor said, "Brishen, you must find a cougar changeling named Kai. He has something. I don't know. The dream…it…" The old man began to tremble violently and tried to sit up. "I don't know the rest, but there is more. Kai, seek him out and—"

"Father, you're not making sense. This is all just a dream. Why would this Kai, if he exists, help the *natsia*?" He looked down at the wrinkled face and again realised how frail the man was. Placing his hands on the bony shoulders, he tried to calm his father's shaking. "Rest, father. We'll talk again in the morning."

Shandor turned his face up and looked into Brishen's eyes. "Kai holds the cougar amulet. Promise me you'll find him. He can help us. Somehow, he can save the horse *natsia*." He took a shuddering breath and collapsed back onto the bed.

"I promise, Father," Brishen vowed.

Shandor's eyes closed, and a soft groan came from him. When he looked up again, he instructed, in a voice that left no room for debate, "Move me now."

Brishen released him and sat looking down at his father. Once a great, powerful leader, Shandor was now little more than the shell of a man. It'd been months since he'd been strong enough to shift into the beautiful black stallion Brishen had watched and revered as he grew.

"Brishen, son," the soft voice of his mother came from the other end of the wagon.

"Yes, I'm still here, mother." He rose to his feet and stepped towards the woman, reaching out a hand to help her in. "He's ready for me to move him."

"He's very weak now." She moved towards the bed and sat on the small stool. Her hand went to her husband's. "Yes, go prepare the canopy."

Brishen did as his parents instructed, making a bed for his father under an improvised canopy in front of their wagon. He carried his father to his final resting spot and made the man as comfortable as possible.

"Thank you for coming," Pesha told him. "He'll rest now. But he was adamant about seeing you tonight."

"He gave me much to think about." Brishen left them alone. He knew they had little time together.

When he had moved out from under the canopy and away from the wagon, he gazed at the star-filled sky. His father's words filled his mind. *'Kai holds the cougar amulet. He can help us. Somehow, he can save the horse natsia.'*

How can a cougar begin to understand the problems of the gypsy horse natsia? Scepticism filled Brishen.

Before he'd taken more than a few paces, he heard a keening wail coming from his mother. He froze and braced himself for the reality of what he knew had happened. Shandor, King of the Gypsy Changelings, was gone.

Even though his heart was filled with sorrow, Brishen thrust out his chest and quickly wiped his eyes. He would not allow the burden of saving the horse *natsia* to shift to strangers. It fell to him, and it was a responsibility he'd accept with pride.

Chapter Two

"Leave me alone!" a child squealed.

Aric dropped the rabbit he was cleaning and raced for the cave where he'd left the little ones playing. "Kasha?" he called frantically as he paused in the doorway.

The little girl, who had her father's soulful black eyes and her mother's beguiling expression, pouted up at him. "Uncle Aric, tell Kale to stop. I found this. It's mine."

"Did not!" The boy made a grab for whatever his sister clutched in her hand. "I saw it first. Give it to me!"

Aric smiled and quickly stepped between the youngsters, who definitely shared their father's zest for excitement. Each sprouted long, dishevelled black hair just like Kai, the man Aric loved more than life. He found it hard to scold them or take sides. But, given that both cougar kits had inherited their mother Sable's spitfire temperaments, adult intervention was sometimes necessary.

He knelt and brushed the hair from Kasha's face. "What have you got there that's so important?"

She opened her fist and displayed a dusty but brilliant purple gemstone. Tarnished yet ornate gold filigree encased the stone.

Astonished, Aric felt the smile melt from him face. "What the..." He blinked then reached for the amulet. "Let me see it, please."

Kasha closed her fist and pulled it to her chest. "It's mine!"

Aric gazed at her patiently. "Sweetheart, I'm afraid you're not going to be able to keep this. Your father needs to see it right away. I think you kits have discovered something very important."

Her lashes fluttered, but she reluctantly handed him the stone.

He took the amulet and studied it. The delicate gold twisted in the shape of an animal's head, and for a moment, he couldn't tell what type. "A horse," he finally whispered, more shocked than ever at the find. There were no horse changelings that he knew of. His cougar clan had encountered bears and wolves, but that was the extent. *Or so we thought.*

Aric stood, palming the amulet. "Time to go."

"Aw, we didn't get to play very long!" Kale complained.

Aric ruffled his hair. "And thanks to you, I didn't get much hunting done. If there's not enough to eat tonight, you're getting seconds on greens."

Kale laughed and ran ahead out of the cave. "You keep saying that, but there's always enough to eat."

Aric smiled. It *was* their normal refrain. He wanted to hunt, and the kits begged to go along then ended up being so noisy they scared away most of the prey. Fortunately, he wasn't the sole provider for the clan. And he did love spending time with his soul-mate's offspring, who affectionately referred to him as 'uncle'.

Kasha's small hand slid into his empty one and squeezed. "After Father sees the stone, do you think I can have it back? I could tie a piece of leather through it and make a wonderful necklace."

Aric scooped her into his arms and nuzzled her warm neck. "I doubt it, little one. The stone is going to make a fine necklace for somebody, but I don't think it'll be a cougar."

"Who, then?" Her eyes lit with wonder.

"We'll leave that up to your father to figure out." He set her down by his pile of partially cleaned rabbits and skins. He wrapped the amulet in a soft pelt and tucked it into one of the three pouches he'd brought. After securing the meat in the other two, he set one in front of each kit. "Time to shift. Each of you, carry a bag—and I expect each of them to make it back to the caves in one piece. No more time to play today. We should hurry. Got it?"

"Yes, Uncle," both kits replied, their faces suddenly serious.

He folded his arms, nodding, and watched their transformations. Both small bodies crouched, backs arched. The muscles in their spines shifted, their arms and legs thickened. Hands and feet morphed into paws with small, sharp claws. Faces elongated, ears moved up, noses slid down. Fur sprouted—shiny black pelts with brown spots, so similar that, at first glance, he could barely differentiate between the littermates. But Kasha bore facial markings like her mother's, and Aric knew the female would eventually grow to be much like the dark-haired beauty who'd borne her.

Aric crouched and began his change. The initial jab of pain quickly shifted to a blissful sense of joy. Human form had its advantages, but there was nothing more exhilarating than being a cat, feral and free. He basked in each sensation as his body morphed, finally coming to rest in the sleek, golden animal guise that truly made him feel alive.

He glanced at the kits who pranced and tumbled around, acclimating to their new forms. He'd give them a minute to stretch and play before they left. He was anxious to get back to Kai. Aric's mind raced with the implications of the kit's discovery, and he wondered what his beloved's reaction might be. *Time to go find out.*

He picked up one pouch in his strong jaws and watched the kits do the same. He headed towards the river, pausing occasionally to make sure Kasha and Kale were still close behind. They never tarried, staying close on his heels.

Pride swelled in his chest. The ornery little buggers had their moments, like all kits, but when it mattered, he was pleased to know he could count on them to behave and follow instructions.

They journeyed swiftly to the clan caves. As they approached the entrance closest to the river, Aric spotted Sable and a couple of other females washing clothes at the water's edge. He drew closer and paused, dropping his bundle to shift back to human form.

Transformation complete, he watched the kits protectively until they, too, had morphed, sprouting gangly arms and legs.

"Mother! Mother!" they shouted in unison, racing to Sable's side.

She bent down and hugged a kit in each arm. Aric admired the swell of her voluptuous breasts as she moved. The full, shapely globes were barely concealed beneath a simple, white cotton shift.

His cock thickened with desire. Sable was the only female to ever inspire that reaction in him. He'd been perfectly happy in his relationship with Kai and hadn't been able to get enough of the man. But when the feisty female entered their lives, she'd added a new dimension neither he nor Kai had expected. Now, they shared their bed with her regularly, and it was bliss for all concerned. More than that, the three shared love and a sense of camaraderie Aric wouldn't exchange for anything. The kits added even more joy to their lives.

He reached for a loincloth that had been draped over a twine clothesline stretched between two trees. Nakedness was commonplace in the shifter community, but there were times when some clothing was prudent. He wrapped the fabric around his hips and tied it at the side.

His attempt at modesty didn't go unnoticed. Over the kit's small, dark-haired heads, Sable gazed at his body and smiled seductively. "How did the hunting go?"

He grimaced. "As far as game, about like you'd expect, merely fair. But the kits made another find. A spectacular discovery I think Kai will be anxious to see."

Her chocolate-brown eyes flashed with apparent interest. "Oh? What's that?"

Aric picked up his bundle and shook the stone from its swaddling. He took it to Sable and held it up for her to see.

He could tell she realised the importance of the find, as he had.

"It's beautiful!" Sable murmured. "Is that a horse?" She pulled her gaze away from the gem and looked into Aric's eyes. "Are there horse shifters?"

He raised his eyebrows questioningly. "None I've ever seen. I thought Kai would want to know about this right away."

"I found it," Kasha said petulantly. "Uncle Aric said I had to give it to father."

Sable stared at the stone for another moment. "Your uncle is right. This is an important discovery, and you were very smart kits to bring it to us." She grabbed two pairs of overalls from the clothesline and helped her young ones dress. Giving each of them a kiss on the cheek, she then shooed them off with swats to the bums. "Go find Ella and ask for a snack. I'll be right there."

"Yes, Mother," both kits replied and scurried off.

Sable lowered her voice. "I'd love to see Kai's expression when you show him this. But I think he's expecting some alone time with you. I'll keep the kits occupied for a while."

Aric grinned. "Thank you."

Her eyes gleamed. "Just don't wear out each other completely. Save a little something for me, later on tonight."

"Always, beautiful." He cupped one of her round arse cheeks and squeezed.

A small moan escaped Sable's lips.

Aric pressed his bundle of rabbit skins into her stomach.

Sable gave him a frustrated look and went to retrieve the game her kits had brought home. With one last, lusty glance over her shoulder at Aric, she followed her youngsters to the communal cave.

Aric trailed after them, only to turn aside and enter the recess he shared with Kai. "Hey, anybody home?"

Kai stepped out from the sleeping alcove, sharpening a knife with a slab of pumice. "Just me. Will I do?"

The sight of Kai's glorious, naked form never failed to arouse Aric. Kai's firm, tanned skin and wide, well-muscled chest made an impressive backdrop for the brilliant bronze stone hanging from his neck.

Aric's gaze dropped lower to the delectable, thick cock which invariably waved at half-staff. The sight took his breath, and he licked his lips. "You're in fine form today, my love. If I didn't have pressing business, I'd be on my knees, sucking you off."

Kai raised an eyebrow. "What could be more important than that?"

With a flick of his wrist, Aric held up the purple amulet. "This."

Kai blinked. His hand trembled when he took the stone and examined it. "Where did you find this?"

"Kasha and Kale uncovered it in the cave near the old ghost town."

"Cato's cave—the cave where the other three amulets were found, many moons ago."

Aric nodded. "I know. What I don't understand is why it turned up now. We've all been in that cave countless times. I've got fine memories of hours whiled away there." He smiled. He and Kai had fucked in every niche in the place at one time or another.

"Were the kits digging?" Kai focussed on the stone.

"I don't think so. It was just there."

Kai continued to study it. "The amulet was meant to be found. Why now? I have no idea. What tribe it belongs to? No idea. I'm not aware of any horse shifters."

"Nor am I." Aric watched his lover's face. "What are you going to do?"

Kai closed his fist around the stone. "Put this in a safe place until I can make some decisions. I may need to call a council meeting of talisman holders. But the journey to bear territory is long. The trek to wolf grounds is even longer. This requires a great deal of thought and planning. I must meditate about it."

Aric stepped closer. "And while you meditate, is there any rule saying I can't suck your cock at the same time?"

Kai smiled. "No, I'm sure there's no rule about that. Just don't make me shoot. I've been thinking about fucking your tight arse all damned day." He turned and entered their sleeping quarters.

Aric followed, watching Kai tuck the purple amulet into a small box. The handsome stud set his knife and sharpening stone down then turned around, stroking his shaft.

With a tug to the string at his hip, Aric let his loincloth fall to the floor. He grasped his own throbbing erection and dragged the skin back and forth. "So, you've been thinking about me, have you? Were you imagining me on my back, legs drawn up, so you could shove that huge monster inside me? Do you plan to pummel me until your balls get nice and tight, and you spew hot, creamy seed deep in my hole?"

Kai maintained eye contact as they each stroked themselves. "That would be nice. Although I do love to press you against the wall and hold one of your legs high so I can drive up into you that way."

Aric grinned. "My love, I'm your loyal servant. Do with me as you will." He dropped to his knees in front of Kai and stared at the man's pre-cum slick erection and the fist wrapped tightly around it. Aric licked his lips before flicking the tip of the cock head. He traced the slit with his tongue, circled the bulbous knob then sucked gently on the crown.

"By the gods," Kai muttered, hips thrusting forward. "That feels good."

"Not too good, remember," Aric teased. He drew the rod deep into his mouth and milked the shaft with his cheeks and tongue. His actions grew firmer, faster, deeper.

Kai ran his hands over Aric's head then rested them on his shoulders. When the ministrations were apparently more than he could bear, he pushed Aric away. "Enough. On your back, golden stud. I need to fuck you."

"Gladly." Aric dropped to their bed of pelts and spread his legs. After wetting two fingers, he reached down and circled the digits around his own anus. The slight pressure felt good, so he inserted them both and fucked them in and out. Then he dragged them from side to side, providing the proper stretching to accept Kai's massive offering. His lover usually took care of that himself, but today Aric sensed electricity and tension in the air. Kai had other things to worry about. The distraction of a nice, hard fuck would do him good. Aric was more then willing to take care of the details.

"Damn, that looks nice." Kai stood above him, stroking his shaft, watching Aric's preparations.

"Ready for a little action?" Aric removed his fingers and raised his arse.

"Do you ever have to ask?" Kai knelt between Aric's legs and pressed the slickened tip to the proffered anus. "I'm ready for action with you any hour of the day."

"Come on," Aric urged, desperate for the warmth of Kai's cock filling his arse. "Don't make me beg. I need you."

Kai drove forward with a groan of pleasure. "Ah, I need you, too, golden warrior." He sank balls-deep and froze. "When we're one like this, my life is complete. Right here is where I should be. Where I crave to be."

"Yes." Aric bucked his hips, straining for more motion. "I feel it, too. We're perfectly mated, you and I. Now, what about that fucking you promised me? Because I saw Sable outside. She seemed willing to take care of whatever problem I had."

Kai thrust into Aric's arse. "Wily wench. We'll take care of her later, when the kits are asleep. I know you love to bury your face between her full, fleshy teats."

Aric could barely think, let alone speak, as his lover pounded into his arse. Indescribable feelings of love and lust flashed through him, and all he wanted to do was explode. Being reminded of Sable's full, round globes with their dark areolas was enough to send him over the edge. "Please!" he gasped.

Kai grasped Aric's cock and squeezed. He stroked it and mumbled, "Come for me, stud."

The delicious pressure was exactly what Aric needed to explode. Satisfaction and pleasure oozed from him, along with several spurts of creamy, warm cum. The blasts coated both their stomachs at the same time Kai's release warmed Aric's rectum.

Their simultaneous orgasms always thrilled Aric. As he peaked, experiencing the ultimate gratification, knowing his lover was sharing those feelings heightened his arousal to the utmost.

It took several minutes for him to catch his breath enough to speak. "Damn," he muttered.

Kai opened his eyes. "My thoughts, exactly. That was incredible."

A throaty, woman's voice came from the doorway. "It looked amazing."

Aric and Kai turned.

Sable entered the alcove, shedding her thin dress and caressing her voluptuous breasts as she approached. "Ella is letting the kits nap in her cave. When I left, they were both sound asleep."

Kai leaned back, pulling slowly from Aric's body. "Then get over here, female. My golden stud has a hankering for teat flesh that only you can satisfy."

Smiling, she climbed on the bed between them. "I was hoping you'd say that. But Kai, I'm dying to know. What are you going to do about the purple amulet?"

"I'm thinking about that," he replied, nuzzling her neck.

"Thinking?" She squirmed under his touch.

"Oh, yes." Aric nodded, trying to look serious. "He's thinking *very hard*."

Kai smiled. "I'll come up with something. There was a reason we were meant to discover the horse amulet. We just have to figure it out. Together, I'm sure we can do it."

"We are good together," Aric agreed, and the threesome smiled.

Chapter Three

Brishen forced down the sob that had threatened ever since his father's body had been burned that morning. His mother, Pesha, was beside herself with sorrow, and he had to be strong for her — and for the others of the *familya*. His father had been king for more years than many could remember, so it was going to be difficult for them all to accustom themselves to his rule.

Rule. The very thought made his heart beat faster. His father had worried that the *natsia* might collapse upon his death. Brishen would not let that happen. He was his father's son, and it was his destiny to take charge.

Other thoughts entered his mind. *Jal.* The man had constantly been at his side, offering his help and a shoulder should Brishen need one. There had been much to prepare, much to do to show Shandor to the final resting place, and Jal had been everywhere helping. More and more, Brishen looked on him as not only a friend, but a companion whom he trusted above all others.

And Tawnie had been there, too, taking care of his mother, making sure the woman ate and rested although sleep evaded the new widow.

While the other women of the *vitsa* cleaned up after the funeral celebration, Tawnie approached him. He was lost in sorrow. Jal had gone out foraging for Mallow, apparently desiring its green leaves in the evening meal. Brishen, sitting on a boulder by the fire, had allowed his mood to sink into the horrible depths of despair and had tried to hide from everyone. She didn't say a word, but suddenly, he felt her hands on his shoulders, her lips on the side of his neck.

"What?" He spun around and faced her, wiping an arm across his eyes to clear the unshed tears from them. Looking up at her, he saw her sadness and realised she was in mourning, too.

"It's all right, Brishen. It's just me." She withdrew her hands and added, "I just wanted to let you know, I'm here for you if you want to talk." She leant down and pressed her lips to his neck again. Somehow understanding his need for solitude, a time to let his grief out alone, she turned and walked back towards the encampment.

"Thank you," Brishen mouthed, but he knew she wouldn't hear him. He truly did need some time to himself. He lurched to his feet and, after looking back at his home, he turned towards the river. His clothes seemed to strangle him, and he shed them as he walked. Rough cotton shirt, boots and finally his jeans were left behind.

He bent forward and brought on the change.

His arms and legs throbbed with an agony that snatched his breath for the duration of a single heartbeat. Euphoria took hold and, as his spine lengthened and his hands and feet morphed, he hit the ground running. The wind pulling at his newly formed mane would have made him smile if his face were capable of it. His eyes shifted to the side, the lower half of his jaw lengthened into a muzzle. His skin itched for a few moments until his coat emerged.

He galloped across the meadow, smelling the clover and new grass. The river came into view, and he raced towards it. In the guise of the horse, Brishen felt completely at ease and let the tears stream from his eyes only to be caught by the wind rushing past. The great wracking sobs came as grunts from deep inside, cleansing him. His hooves pounded into the soft loam, dirt flying up behind him in his wild dash for the river bank.

The long grass gave way to random trees then the rocks and gravel of the riverside. Brishen slowed his pace to a trot, then a walk, and let his head fall forward. The rich smell of clover filled his nostrils, and he snorted his pleasure. Tears done, his heart felt lighter now that he'd allowed some of his grief to leave him. His father would have wanted that.

Thirsty, he entered the icy cold river and sucked up the refreshing water until he had his fill. The near freezing liquid felt good on his ankles and legs, so he walked down river for a while, letting his thoughts go back to Jal.

He clambered onto the shore and found a grassy area where he could lie down. Folding his legs, he rolled onto his back, wriggled mightily and groaned with pleasure. Satisfied he'd scratched everything scratchable, he righted himself and tucked his forelegs under his chest.

The image of Jal's black flesh crept into his thoughts, and his cock stirred. Lying on his side, he began the shift back into human form. Although he loved the guise of a horse, he wanted hands. The sudden flash of pain sent a shudder along his spine. Then bliss took over, and he groaned again, his thoughts going to the daydreams he'd had about Jal. The man's body excited him, the wide shoulders and the broad chest, his long, muscular legs and all the things between.

His change complete, Brishen rolled onto his back, naked, and gazed up. Fluffy clouds moved slowly across the sky. A flock of geese honked their way towards the swamp he knew lay to the east.

Jal's face filled his thoughts, the strong jaw, the high brow, the hawk-like nose and the full lips he'd love to kiss. Groaning, he pushed that thought aside and clenched his fists at his sides to keep from stroking the erection growing at his middle.

Is my attraction to Jal so wrong?

He rolled onto his stomach and pushed himself up onto his elbows. He plucked a piece of grass then stuck the soft end of it into his mouth and chewed thoughtfully. He knew he was expected to father several children. As the future king, he had to be sure the line of succession was strong. His father had chosen Tawnie for him. Her kindness and willingness to help anyone who needed it were always appreciated. And, she had a way with children that he adored. Often he'd seen her surrounded by youngsters, playing or teaching them, it didn't matter. He had to admit he found her very attractive. Her lush curves made his heart race. Yet, thoughts of fucking Jal took his breath.

His hips jerked. His cock, hard as granite, slid across the grass.

"Fuck!" He turned over and glared up at the clouds. The birds were long gone, and that left him an erection and Jal to ponder. Add the last things his father had talked about, and he felt like his head was going to explode. Kai, a cat changeling who'd be able to help the horse *natsia* survive. How could that be?

He pushed that aside and focused his thoughts on Jal. A much nicer topic, and this time, he let his hand roam. His own hips and thighs were tightly muscled, and the ridges rippled across his belly when he reached down towards his crotch. The crinkled hair around the base of his cock tickled his palm. When his fingers slid around his shaft, his balls lifted towards his body.

The roughness of his palm added to the shuddering thrill racing along his spine. Every nerve ending in his body felt charged with electricity. A gentle stroke from base to tip sent his mind into high gear, imagining someone else's hand, firm, strong, a man's hand, touching him. Brishen tightened his grip and stroked himself again, dragging the skin back to the tip of his erection. His shaft pulsed, and pre-cum oozed over his fingers. Spreading his legs, he reached down with his free hand and cupped his balls.

"Yesss!" His hips thrust up, and sweat ran down his sides to mingle with the grass beneath him. He ran his palm over the tip of his cock then back down to the base.

"That looks delicious!"

Brishen's eyes sprang open, and he sat up. Still gripping his cock, more to hide it now than to continue his masturbation, he peered around until he spotted Jal a few paces away.

"What the hell are you doing here?" He turned to the side, embarrassed at being caught—but, even more, confused by the sudden rush of excitement.

"I was worried about you."

Jal, as naked as Brishen, took a step closer. So used to seeing skin, it wasn't until Jal came a little closer that Brishen noticed the man's ebony cock jutting towards him, as hard and dripping as his own. His eyes remained there until Jal stopped only a pace or so away.

"Like what you see?" The black skinned man wiggled his hips, sending his cock flailing from side to side.

Dry mouthed, Brishen pushed aside the response he wanted to make about how much he liked what he saw and instead croaked, "Worried? Wha…"

"Yes, worried. You left without saying where you were going." A dark fleshed hand moved to the shaft of that ebony column and gripped it tightly. "I was hoping to comfort you…if that's what you need."

Brishen blinked and shook his head, trying to regain some composure. When he opened his eyes again, Jal was still there and still caressing himself. It took all the strength he had not to leap on the man. Years of denial and desire seemed to crush him.

"Are you all right?" The note of concern was quite evident in Jal's voice.

When Jal released his erection and leaned down towards him, Brishen lost the battle he'd fought for so many years. Reaching out, he slid his hand behind Jal's neck and pulled the man's face closer to his own. "No, I'm not all right. I…" Words failed him, but he was too far gone to stop. With just the tiniest pressure, Jal's lips touched his.

Hot breath against his cheek and the scent of clover filled his senses.

Brishen let go of his cock and reached for Jal's, so temptingly near. The man's shaft jumped in his grasp, and he tightened his grip. Jal's erection felt so different from his own. Harder, thicker, yet like satin against his palm. Brishen forced down his crazed desire to suck it, to nibble its length and taste the pre-cum oozing over his fingers.

"Don't stop. By the gods, you're going to make me shoot," Jal whispered huskily, his lips still touching Brishen's.

Filled with his father's lectures about bringing more young into the *vitsa,* guilt tore at Brishen. Tawnie, the chosen one, leapt into his thoughts—her lush curves, the sweet scent of her breath when they'd kissed and her caring nature. Yet, the harder body, the more muscular frame had him panting for more.

He increased his stroking, revelling in the way Jal's breath caught and his body jerked to meet the stroke. The cock pulsed and grew even harder in his fist. The man's balls rose up, bumping against the back of Brishen's hand, the wiry hair tickling even more than his own had a while ago. He wanted to see Jal come. He wanted to feel the sticky cum on his chest and belly.

He broke their kiss and looked deep into Jal's eyes. There, he was sure he saw more than friendship, more than the caring of one man for another. Lust was there in plenty, but it wasn't just that.

"Come for me," Brishen whispered, barely able to admit how much he wanted to experience the man's climax.

The hint of a smile on Jal's face turned to a gasp of pleasure as his body jerked. His eyes closed, his hips thrust into Brishen's hand, and he gave a final growl of bliss as a long stream of white shot from his cock.

"Yes, that's it," urged Brishen, more turned on than he could remember feeling for a very long time. His father's wishes set aside for the moment, lust raged within him. He thrust out his chest and belly, making sure the next creamy emission landed on his body. He inhaled the rich, musky scent of the man and tucked it away for future reference.

Then the guilt of their encounter re-emerged. His father's wishes that he mate and reproduce for the good of the clan reared up. Yet, how could this feeling, the caring offer of love, be so wrong?

Confused, Brishen finished Jal off and released the man's cock. He wiped his hand on the grass, cleaning it of the sticky cream. He couldn't bear to look into Jal's eyes again until the man tucked his fingers beneath his chin and forced his face up.

"What's the matter?" Jal's tone was soft, yet firm.

"This is wrong," Brishen blurted. "Father wanted me to take Tawnie as mate. He often talked about grandsons and bringing up the numbers of our *vitsa*."

"How could this be wrong? I care for you, my sexy stud. I would never do anything to hurt you, or our *natsia*. You know that." Jal knelt and leant forward, pressing a kiss to Brishen's lips. "I've loved you for as long as I can remember. I will always love you, but I will never force you to do anything you don't want."

So many emotions tore at Brishen, he couldn't take it in, not right then. He felt as if his head were going to explode. When Jal slid his arms around him, he sank into them gratefully and simply held on.

"It's hard to believe my father's gone." Brishen's cheek lay against Jal's shoulder, his lips nearly brushing the man's ear. "He's been king for longer than most of us can remember."

"That's true. Maybe it's time for some new blood. We both know his illness has kept him from being the ruler the *natsia* has needed the last few months."

"That last night, just before he died, we spoke." Brishen eased away from Jal and settled cross-legged on the grass. "He told me about a dream he had. A very strange dream."

Jal sat beside him and also crossed his legs, their knees touching. "What kind of dream? They say that a dying person's dreams sometimes have great meaning."

Brishen cocked his head sideways and peered at Jal. "You believe that?"

"I don't know. I can't say it's not true. But I remember stories about when my Grandmare died. She said there'd be one more death in the family before she was buried. The very next day, my uncle was killed in a freak rockslide."

"Coincidence," Brishen said, but he shuddered.

"Maybe. But it happened." Jal slipped his arm around Brishen's waist and pulled him closer. "What was your father's dream?"

Brishen took a deep breath before going on. "It was about other changeling clans and how I'm supposed to find someone named Kai, a cougar man. He's supposed to have some knowledge about how to save our *vitsa* and maybe even the *natsia.*"

"Interesting. But how are you supposed to find this Kai?"

"No idea, he didn't give directions." Brishen repeated to Jal the complete story as best as he could remember. He told him about the amulets and how Cato found them and made sure they all went to the right owners. It took the better part of the afternoon to fill him in and answer the man's questions. "And when I left, mother went in to sit with him. He was very weak, and I knew he wouldn't last much longer."

"So, he just told you about this once?"

"Yes, just that one time." He remembered vividly the crying howl his mother had made when his father died.

"An amulet that can give you power."

"Not necessarily me. The amulet will go to the rightful holder, the true leader. At least that's what I got from father's ranting."

"I can't think of a better leader than you, my sexy stud."

"I have no mate. If the story's to be believed, the stone only goes to one who's with his life partner. That person must also have the good of the *natsia* in her heart."

"Or *his* heart." Jal smiled. "Perhaps the amulet will know you have someone who loves you and cares for you more than life. Perhaps it will know this someone has the good of all the *vitsas* in his heart."

Brishen shook his head. "Right now, I don't feel much like a king or even like anyone who could possibly hope to hold a talisman with the kind of power father spoke of."

"Give yourself time. Grieve for your father, then we'll talk some more."

Brishen turned his face towards Jal just as the man was about to kiss him on the neck. Their faces bumped, and their lips found each other's. For an instant, Brishen

161

panicked. *My father. I have to abide by my father's wishes. Or do I?*

His cock, which had deflated while they talked, again rose up, stiff and hard. Jal's fingers circled it, gripped it and gently tugged at the turgid flesh, but after only a moment of sheer bliss, Brishen pushed the man's hand away. "Please, let me mourn. I need time to think before I'll feel right about this."

Jal released him and slipped his hand along the smooth expanse of Brishen's thigh. "Time we have. All the time in the world. I won't rush you. Just remember, I want you. No matter what happens, I want you and I love you."

Brishen looked into the man's eyes and whispered, "Yes, I know. I think I might feel the same way, but I need time. I have to decide what's right not only for the *vitsa* but for the *natsia.*"

Smiling, Jal nodded. "Yes, and that will be right for you, and for me."

Both men looked up as the soft thud of hoof beats approached them. Tan bodied and nearly white of mane and tail, Tawnie drew their attention as she neared. Her change took only a few moments, and both men waited silently while her human form emerged.

"I thought I'd find you two together," she said when she straightened. She smiled and moved closer, her woman scent mingling with the masculine aroma of men lusting. "I can go if you'd like privacy."

Her offer touched Brishen's heart. "No. Join us, Tawnie."

She sank to her knees before him then wriggled to his side. They formed a kind of triangle, and each wrapped their arms around two of the others.

Tawnie's soft skin felt amazing against his. Jal's muscular body took his breath. A glimmer of peace showed itself.

"Are you all right, Brishen?" Tawnie looked into his eyes.

"Yes. And I need to tell you about the dream my father had just before he died." As soon as the words left his mouth, the glimmer of peace spread. Something was right, something important.

Chapter Four

Aric bent and sniffed the grass at the edge of the clearing. The wide, sunny meadow looked innocent enough, but from experience, he knew better than to dash across without taking precautions. The tips of the tall blades waved in the soft breeze, but nothing more. The brush across from him was silent. Even the red tailed hawk he saw floating above gave up its perusal of the area and veered to the south.

Aric's tail remained low, and the golden fur at the nape of his neck stood on end. Senses on high alert, he crept forward cautiously into the clearing. There were reasons changeling cougars didn't venture far from clan territory.

The biggest concern was man. The humans from Newburgen and surrounding towns were avid hunters. Kai didn't want any of his family ending up a stuffed trophy, and Aric heartily agreed.

The second problem was a little trickier to manage. Other animals hunted these grounds. Aric wasn't interested in becoming someone's dinner, either. The farther he strayed from his home, the more cautious he became. If he understood Kai's descriptions accurately, Aric now ventured into bear territory.

He'd met the bear talisman holder once, about a year prior. The muscular, bald man had actually saved his hide, and on that day both he and Kai had pledged eternal gratitude to the handsome, dark-skinned man, Tarek.

Kai had instructed Aric to seek out Tarek, the bears' tribal leader, and his mate, Skye. He'd know Terek by the shiny, blue amulet around his neck, the symbol of his place among all changelings. Unfortunately, without Kai and his golden amulet by Aric's side, travelling through unknown territory was extremely dangerous. His journey was important, though, a risk that had to be taken. Kai would never have sent him otherwise.

Aric crept through the tall grass, staying low, until he caught the musky odour of something feral. His sense of smell was immensely better than any human could dream of. His ability to communicate, on the other hand, was next to impossible in this form.

I'm close. Time to change.

He shrugged the pack from his shoulders and tucked his head in, beginning the transformation. Slowly, precisely, his spine shifted and bones contorted, adjusting. A quick thrill zipped through his core as he marvelled, like always, about the amazing way his body morphed from one being into another. The excitement of the change never ceased to steal his breath for one, brief moment. When fur had been absorbed into smooth, tanned skin, he stood up and stretched.

Aric pulled a soft, cotton shirt and dark pants from his pack and dressed. After tugging a pair of soft-soled boots onto his feet, he pulled his long, blond hair into a ponytail and secured it with strip of leather. Satisfied, he closed his knapsack and shouldered it.

He drew closer, the musky odour growing stronger. *The bear camp.* He glanced around quickly. If the bears were anything like his cougar clan, there'd be someone on guard to warn when strangers neared the encampment. Aric only hoped the watchman would be in human form so they could communicate. He took another step forward then paused when the bushes rustled in front of him.

Before he had time to think, a tall, muscular man stepped from behind the nearest sturdy tree and stopped in front of him.

"Afternoon, stranger." The man wore nothing but a loincloth. A beaded necklace ornamented his tanned, naked chest.

Aric dragged away his gaze from the spectacular physique and looked at the man's face. Handsome, with a chiselled jaw line and cheeks, he sported shoulder-length, brown hair and dark chocolate irises to match. A tight smile curled his lips upwards at the edges, but the affable expression didn't quite reach his eyes.

"Hello, friend." Aric kept his gaze on the spectacular stud. "Perhaps you can tell me if I'm in the right place. I seek a man named Tarek. I was given to understand this was his territory."

The sexy face lit up with apparent interest. He puffed his chest out. "What business do you have with Tarek?"

Aric maintained eye contact. He felt quite sure he'd arrived at Tarek's camp. The other man was being properly cautious, something all changelings were forced to do, especially with various towns so close to all their lands. "Talisman business. I was sent by Kai, ruler of the cougar tribe."

The man studied Aric, giving him a careful once over. "We've heard of Kai. And you would be..."

"I'm Aric, his partner. Actually, Kai and I met Tarek about a year ago. He and his mate, Skye, appeared at a particularly opportune moment."

"Really?" He folded his arms across his chest. "Unfortunately, Skye met with an untimely accident. I am Tarek's mate, now. I'm Raven."

"Pleased to meet you."

Raven continued to watch him warily, though the caution in his dark eyes slowly turned to interest. "You said something about our talisman?"

His piercing gaze sent a spark of energy sizzling through Aric. "Not *your* talisman, specifically. A new amulet has been discovered. Kai hopes to meet with Tarek and the leader of the wolf clan, whoever that might be, to discuss the implications."

"Fascinating." Raven glanced towards his camp. "Come with me. I'll take you to Tarek."

"Thank you." Aric followed him through the brush until they came upon a clearing. A circle of half a dozen tipis surrounded a rock fire pit in the middle. A few people went about their daily chores, some clothed, some naked. The place felt, surprisingly, a lot like where he came from. "Nice camp," he murmured for lack of better words.

"Home, sweet home." Raven walked to the farthest tent and, after tapping on the support pole, opened the flap. "Tarek? We have a guest."

Aric looked in and spotted the man he remembered, lying on a bed of pelts. Naked but for the brilliant blue amulet resting on his chest, Tarek was not alone. Another man, with long black hair and brown skin, stretched out next to him. They were head to toe, an advantageous position for what they seemed to be doing. *Playing with each other's cocks.* Aric inhaled, wondering how Raven, Tarek's supposed mate, would react.

"His name's Aric," Raven said in what seemed a nonchalant manner. "Says he was sent by the cougar tribe leader."

Tarek leant back, one hand lazily stroking his partner's thick, coffee-coloured erection. He set his gaze on Aric, and his eyes sparkled. "Aric! I remember. The last time we met, you were hanging above a ravine."

"I'm only here today because of your selflessness." Aric bowed his head respectfully. He tried to ignore the fact that the tribal leader continued playing with another man's dick while they spoke. "Kai sends his regards."

"Ah, yes. Kai. Strong warrior, that one. You both are." Tarek sent one last, yearning glance at his lover's shaft before releasing it. He sat up, reached for a loincloth and draped it around his waist as he stood. He motioned to the man getting up from the other side of the bed. "This is my partner, Inuka. I see you've met Raven, our third."

A triad. Aric smiled, understanding dawning on him. As much as he enjoyed Sable's luscious breasts, adding a third man to his lovemaking with Kai sounded like an intriguing idea. He nodded in greeting to the man known as Inuka, another handsome spectacle with a muscular physique and shining, black hair.

"Cougar tribe, you say?" Inuka tied a loincloth around his hips. "What are you doing so far from home?"

"An important discovery brings me to you." Aric looked at Tarek. "A fourth amulet. We found it in the cave where the original three talismans were discovered by Cato so long ago."

Tarek's dark eyes widened. "Another amulet? What species does it portray?"

"Horses. It's purple with the head of a stallion in the gold filigree."

Tarek fingered his own amulet as he paced back and forth in front of Aric. "Horses. Astounding. I've never encountered horse changelings."

"Kai's thoughts exactly. We've never met any horse shifters. We've actually never come face to face with any of the wolves, either, though we know roughly where they're supposed to be."

"I've seen the wolves a few times. Last year, when the fire raged through the forest, we encountered a few of them. I understand they lost their tribal leader at that time."

The words shook Aric to the core. "That's a shame." He hated to hear of a fallen amulet bearer, regardless of what tribe he ruled. "Hopefully they've chosen a new leader, by now."

"I'm sure they have." Tarek smiled. "The amulet chooses, you know. In the case of the wolves, I believe it chose a pup who hadn't sown all the wild oats he seemed to think he needed to. It'll be interesting to see how that worked out."

Aric nodded. "If you could direct me to their dens, I'd appreciate it. I need to carry Kai's message to whoever their leader is. Kai's hoping the three talisman-holders can meet in a week at the old ghost town near Newburgen. There's a cave nearby where the amulets were found. Kai believes if we put all our heads together, we can figure out what to do about the new amulet and decide where it belongs."

"I know the ghost town and the cave that you mean." Tarek glanced at each of his lovers. "My partners and I will be there. Sending you off to find the wolves is a slightly more complicated task if you're not familiar with the area."

Raven spoke up quickly. "I'll take him. We can make the journey in less than a day, if we shift."

Surprised, Aric looked at the brown-haired man.

Before he could protest, Tarek smiled and said, "Agreed. Some might find it amusing to see a bear and a cougar travelling together — especially if they have little packs on their backs."

"I couldn't show up here naked," Aric protested. Clothing was lost when a shifter went from one form to another. The only way to ensure it made the trip was to remove it and carry it.

"Sure you could have." Raven waggled his eyebrows at Aric.

Aric rubbed his hands together, nerves suddenly rattled. He wasn't concerned about making the trip with a bear. Just one particular bear — *Raven*. They were different creatures, yet in human form, all too similar. *And too fucking tempting*. He scrambled to make up a lie. "This is very kind of you, really. But time is of the essence, and I think it'd be faster if —"

Raven broke into a grin. "What, you think a bear can't keep pace with a cougar?" He laughed uproariously.

Deep rumbles shuddered from his two partners as they joined in his merriment.

Aric's face heated with an embarrassed flush. "I, uh, ah, shit."

Raven stepped so close, Aric could feel the man's breath on his face. "Bears are more agile than you might think." He looked up and down Aric's body then slowly walked behind him.

A light touch moved Aric's ponytail, then the warm breath brushed his shoulder.

Raven murmured, "If you'd like to place a wager on who has more stamina, I'm willing."

Aric gulped. He was surprised when Tarek laughed again. The big man crossed his arms over his chest and shook his head. "I'm not sure it's wise to send my mate on a journey with you, Golden Boy. We don't see many males with your colouring in these parts. I think my Raven is quite enamoured."

"Now, look." Aric raised his hands. "I'm not here to—"

"Take it easy." Raven strode around in front of him, a smile planted firmly on his face. "I'm just yanking your chain. I'll take you to wolf territory and see that you get safely back to your home when we're done. But you've had a long journey, already. You should take a meal with us and get some rest. We'll leave at daybreak, if that's all right."

Uneasy relief settled in Aric's gut, and he nodded. The handsome man might have been teasing, but the look in his eyes said *pure lust.* "I'd be grateful for a meal," Aric finally acknowledged. "And a safe place to lay my head."

"You'll be safe here." Tarek walked past them and chuckled at Raven. "Safe enough, anyway. Come. I'd like to hear more about the purple amulet and its discovery."

Aric followed him out, slipping past the grinning Raven. Teasing or not, the man still looked at him like a meal he'd been starving for. Aric wasn't interested in the least, but he couldn't deny a niggle of temptation at the stud's dark, good looks.

It's going to be a long night.

* * * *

Aric slunk through the grass behind the large, brown bear. They'd been travelling for the better part of the day, and Raven had proven himself correct. In the guise of a bear, he moved more quickly than Aric would have expected and did *not* lack for stamina. They'd stopped once for a quick meal of rabbit but had been on the go the rest of the day.

Just as Aric caught a whiff of a musky scent, Raven paused. He rose on his rear paws and shrugged the pack from his back. They made eye contact just before the bruin began to shift.

Aric tossed off his own pack and proceeded to change. *We're close.* Relief seeped through him. The journey hadn't been as dangerous with the accompanying bear, but it was still long and tiring. He was ready to get it over with and go home.

"Ahh!" Raven groaned and stretched out his human limbs. He shook his arms and paced a bit on newly formed legs. "Feels good to shift back."

The comment amused Aric, who stood to get his own bearings as a man. He usually felt that way about his sleek cat form which, in some ways, was more comfortable than the man guise. "I like being a cougar. There's nothing like the freedom of racing through the woods on four feet, and my senses are so much sharper in the feline form."

Raven ran a hand over his smooth, muscular arm. "I like being a bear, too. But it's not about the freedom, so much. There's amazing strength and power in being such a big animal."

Of course. The bears were massive, bulky creatures. Aric could understand why the lighter-weight human forms might be preferable to them at times. He cast a quick glance over the striking, naked man. Raven's cock stood at half-staff, and Aric would swear he saw a glistening drop of pre-cum on the tip.

"See anything you like?" The smiling man took a step towards him. Raven's eyes roamed Aric's body, his gaze pausing at his mid-section. "Because I do." The bear of a man grasped his own shaft and stroked it as he approached.

Aric's erection lengthened and hardened. He took a step back. *This is not what Kai sent me here for.* The brown-haired hunk was an amazing specimen with a thick cock that Aric would love to get a taste of. *But I love Kai, more.* A deep, unfailing love that hadn't lessened over time. Just a glimpse of his beautiful man, or cat, took his breath away every time. "Raven, stop. I'm not sure this is a good idea. As appealing as you are, my heart belongs to Kai."

Raven smiled, still stroking his length. "And my heart lies with Tarek. But this is something different. I've never been with a man from another species, and the thought alone nearly gets me off. Tarek would be the first one to tell me to go for it. He understands pure, animal lust."

"But we're not animals now, are we?" Aric smiled at him sadly. "In this form, I feel bound to the loyalties of men."

Raven laughed. "You think men are loyal creatures? You are naïve, Aric."

"Maybe. But I choose to be true to Kai, my leader and my love."

Raven took a step back. "Your Kai is a lucky man." He gave one last pull to his erection then released it with a sigh of apparent regret.

"Tarek seems like a good mate," Aric offered.

Raven reached for his pack and drew out the clothing he'd stuffed inside. As he dressed, he replied, "Tarek is amazing. I couldn't ask for a better partner." He slipped into his boots and stood upright, smiling. "But we're a horny lot. You'll have to forgive me for trying."

Aric laughed and dressed quickly. "Nothing to forgive. I appreciate your bringing me here. There's safety in numbers."

"True." Raven shouldered his pack. "Shall we go see if the wolves agree?"

"Sure." Aric followed Raven, who took long, no-nonsense strides.

At the base of a cliff, they encountered two small, blond-haired children playing in the grass. The smaller of the two, a little female, blinked up at them as they approached. "Tad. Look!" she squealed.

The pup, who looked so much like the female he had to be her brother, blinked his surprise. He faced them, hands on hips. "Who are you?" he demanded with a voice that didn't match his bravado.

Aric smiled. "We're looking for a man named Cole. We heard he was the tribal leader of the...pack." He left out the word 'wolf' in case they were in the wrong place. The children were cute. They reminded him of Kasha and Kale. He didn't want to frighten them.

"My father is Cole," the boy announced thrusting out his chest.

"Does he wear the red amulet?" Raven asked.

Tad's small face took on a concerned look, his brow wrinkling. "How do you know about that?"

"Good." Aric smiled and nodded at Raven. "We need to see—"

"Daisy, go get father! Hurry!" the boy called to his playmate.

She scampered off with a high-pitched squeal. "Father! Father!"

"Wait, calm down." Aric held his hands out to the boy. "We don't mean you any harm. We simply need to speak with him."

The loud rustling of brush at the base of the cliff told Aric more than one person was headed towards them. Three adults appeared behind the boy, who was scooped up by a tall man with long, black hair. With a swat to the child's bum, he sent the boy scooting back towards his sister, tucked safely away behind them. He folded his arms across his chest and looked at the two new arrivals. "You've stumbled across private property, gentlemen. Can I direct you back to the nearest road?"

Aric caught a glimpse of the sparkling, red amulet beneath the man's leather jerkin. He smiled with relief. This one seemed reasonable, someone they could talk with. The other two men, one young, tall, with long, pale, almost white hair, and the other, older yet muscular, both bore spears. "You'd be Cole?"

The dark-haired man squinted. He examined Aric's face. "I don't know you." Turning his gaze to Raven, he said, "You are familiar. Where have we met?"

"Sir." Raven bowed his head respectfully. "After the fire last year, I believe it was you who helped bury my uncle." He glanced at the white-haired warrior then back at Cole. "I am Raven, of the bear changeling tribe."

"Yes!" Cole turned to the man at his side and pushed the spear down. "You remember him, Zane. We found them shortly after we found the body of our own tribal leader, Gar."

"Of course." Zane nodded, lowering his weapon.

Cole motioned to the older man who had also dropped his spear to his side. "This is my uncle, Kaleb." He looked at Aric. "And you are..."

Aric gave a small nod of respect. "I am Aric, mate to Kai, ruler of the cougar tribe."

Cole chuckled. "A cougar and a bear together? I hope you're not coming to tell me the sky is falling. I've got far too much living to do yet."

"Nothing quite that serious, but important all the same," Aric replied. "Kai sends his regards along with news that a fourth amulet has been discovered. A purple horse talisman."

"Horses?" Kaleb, the eldest of the trio, seemed the first to understand the significance of the discovery. "Horse changelings? Have you seen these beings?"

"No." Aric shook his head. "We were hoping you could offer some insight. Kai would like the talisman holders to meet in the ghost town near Newburgen in a week to discuss this matter."

Cole glanced from his uncle to Zane then back at Aric. "We might have some useful knowledge. Zane and I actually saw some wild horses one day, not all that far from here."

"Yes," Zane agreed. "We thought it was unusual at the time, but perhaps it now makes sense."

Enthusiasm raced through Aric. This was precisely the type of information Kai was looking for. *My trip has been worthwhile.* "Can I tell my leader that you'll meet us at the cave by the ghost town?"

"Absolutely." Cole beckoned them forward. "But, please. You've come a long way. Take supper with us and share our fire for the night before you start back."

"We'd be happy to do so." Aric smiled at Raven, who had to be as exhausted as he was but might not admit it.

"Yes. Thank you," Raven agreed.

"A purple amulet, you say?" Kaleb motioned them in the direction of the wolf den, and they all walked. "I'm bursting to know more about it."

"I'll gladly tell you what I know." Relief filled Aric. Kai had done the right thing by sending him on this journey. Now, he was anxious to get back and tell his leader what he'd found. He was also more than a little eager to jump the man's bones. A nice, earth-rattling fuck would be the perfect welcome home. Adrenaline and arousal oozed through Aric at the thought, and he smiled.

Chapter Five

Brishen leant down and pressed his lips to Tawnie's. For the past several days they'd engaged in sensual fondling and long, warm kisses. As much as he wanted to be with the male who had stolen his heart, he desired Tawnie, too. His life was topsy-turvy, but he somehow knew she was destined to be part of it, as was Jal.

The sweet taste of her excited him tremendously. His erection pulsed between their bodies. It was time for the next step. He ached to make love to Tawnie, and could tell she felt the same way.

When he finally broke the connection of their mouths, he gasped a huge sigh and looked down into her dark brown eyes.

"I hope it's all right for us to be here, Brishen," she said, a note of concern making her voice tremble. "I know you and Jal..."

"Jal and I have something special, it's true." He wondered what she thought of them, yet couldn't expect her to understand why he was so unsure of himself. "But you and I also share a bond, Tawnie. I want to be here with you. I desire you. I...*need* you."

"Good." She snuggled against him, her hand tightening around his firm erection. "Because I want to be with you, too." She gave his cock a healthy squeeze.

He shuddered then reached around to cup her arse cheeks in his hands. The smooth expanse of soft flesh filled his palms and more. Their softness thrilled him, yet something felt not right. The pressure of her tits against his chest made him shiver with desire, but he yearned for Jal's hard, masculine muscles.

Her grip slid down his shaft to the base, and he groaned with pleasure. She knew how to excite him, that was for sure. Even with her too soft body, his lust grew. He cared for Tawnie, deeply. His father had paired them, and in the depths of his mind, Brishen wanted to honour the man's wishes. That wasn't all, though. He had grown to admire her courage and her love for everyone in the *vitsa*. She was truly a magnificent woman. Yet, his thoughts of Jal left him confused.

Rolling over, he pulled the dark-eyed beauty atop him. Her thighs parted, and her grip on his shaft tightened even more. "Yes, this is exactly where I wish to be." She smiled down at him and stroked his length.

"You're beautiful," Brishen whispered, trying to keep from thrusting into her hand.

Her fist slid up his shaft, bumped the ridge then slipped down again to his balls. "Love me, Brishen."

He lost his battle, and his hips lurched upwards, nearly sending the woman flying. He gripped her waist, holding her in place before going on.

She rose up, clearing his mid-section just enough to allow her to drag his cock back and rub its head against her wetness. The soft, downy hair tickled him, tormented him, in the strangest way imaginable. The slick petals of her cunt dragged over him, anointing him with their essence.

"Fuck me. I want to know what it feels like to have you deep inside me. I need you."

He reached up and took hold of her tits, one large mound to a hand, and squeezed them. Flesh bulged between each finger. He pressed his thumbnails into the nipples, drawing a guttural groan from her.

"Yes, I need it, too," he sighed and, using her breasts as handles, dragged her down onto his throbbing cock. Her tightness resisted, but slowly his cock filled her. The sensation proved to be nearly too much for him, and he gritted his teeth to keep from spewing his load at once.

Her groans turned him on even more. When she clenched her pussy, he thought he'd died and gone to Nirvana. He held completely still, willing himself to think of something else, anything, to keep from coming. It worked, and when she settled down on his thighs, he sighed with relief.

"You feel so big," she mumbled and leant forward, placing her hands on his shoulders. "You're throbbing inside me. It's amazing."

"And I can feel you clenching. Keep it up, and I'll come," he warned her, but smiled to reassure her. "You're so hot and tight. It's incredible."

"You're making me crazy. I've wanted this for weeks. Fuck me." She ground her pubes into his, clenching herself around his pulsing shaft as if trying to milk him.

He shuddered and tightened the muscles of his bum, straining to control the sudden blinding need to shoot.

"Fuck. Damn," he mumbled nearly incoherently. He dug his fingers into her thighs and held her as still as he could. "Tawnie, stop, or I swear I'll come."

The woman chuckled and leant down to kiss him. Again, her lips were like the softest of silk, her tongue a wet digit searching for his. She tasted of wildness and desire.

Fingers tight, he churned his hips, grinding into her with abandon. As long as he controlled the movement, he felt as if he could keep from sending his seed deep into her core. He pulled her up, stopping only when he felt the delicate folds of her cunt fluttering around the head of his cock. He held her there, high above him, while kissing and nipping at her tongue. She struggled, obviously trying to sink down on him, and he finally relented.

"Bastard," she moaned into his mouth.

"Yeah, I know," he replied in as soft a tone. "Don't see you scurrying away. Must like it."

"Yes, you beast." Tawnie sat up and smiled down at him.

Her hair hung in long waves, concealing her neck and part of her chest but leaving her nipples bare. Tight nubbins, a deep rose colour, stood proudly from the centre of each breast. He reached for them with fingers and thumbs, eager to toy with them. Her moan as he lightly pinched them drove him to even greater teasing. He twisted one, then the other, then both together. Lifting her entire breasts, he jiggled the mounds until she reached for his hands.

He loved the play, yet, something niggled at him. Too soft. Not tight enough. Too frail.

He spread his fingers, taking each breast in hand and squeezing them until Tawnie gasped. A slight furrow appeared on her brow, a frown to her lips.

"What's wrong, Brishen?" She placed her hands over his and stroked his fingers, his wrists, until he loosened his grip.

He released the tempting mounds of woman flesh, the softness slipping from his hands.

She worked the muscles in her cunt, the slick sheath pulling at him like nothing he'd ever experienced before.

"What's wrong, my sweet beast?"

He gazed up at her and tried a smile. Even to himself, it felt not quite right—yet perhaps it was. He wanted her. Thoughts of Jal surfaced, but only for a moment. She was perfect for him, and he knew it deeply. "Nothing. I'm sorry." He stroked her sides, carefully, tenderly, and murmured, "Did I hurt you?"

"No, you could never do that." She looked into his eyes and frowned. "There is something wrong, isn't there?"

Brishen would have given anything to deny it, but he couldn't, and she seemed to know it. He slipped his hands along her sides, enjoying her smoothness, yet still feeling as if it weren't quite right. He pulled her down. When she was nicely settled against his chest, his erection still buried happily in the warmth of her cunt, he whispered, "There's nothing wrong with you. You're adorable, sexy as hell and..." He lost the words and pressed his face into her hair.

"It's Jal, isn't it?" Her breath brushed the light fuzz on his chest.

"Yes, sort of, I think," he murmured, then smiled at his discomfort. Inhaling, he chastised himself silently while enjoying the scent of her long, silken tresses.

"It's all right, you know. To care for Jal, I mean," Tawnie whispered barely loud enough for him to hear.

He cupped her arse cheeks and one more time thrust into her. His cock didn't seem to care much for his feelings as long as it had a warm place to find its pleasure. *But, I do care for this woman.* "Yes, I know. Except my father had other plans. The *vitsa* needs a strong leader now more than ever. And one who will give them heirs."

His cock pulsed, and for a moment, he allowed himself to sink into the pleasure.

"True, but there's more than one way to form a bond."

He worked himself into her, gently fucking her while caressing the smooth expanse of her female curves.

"And there are women who are willing to share their man," she continued.

He kissed her nipple and murmured, "But they often wind up warring between them."

"Who knows what the future will bring? Happiness has to be worked for, it's not an easy thing."

Brishen looked up into her eyes. "It seems you've given this some thought."

"Yes, I'm not entirely blind. I see how you look at Jal—how he looks at you."

Brishen's smile turned into a chuckle. "I guess I'm not as good at keeping secrets as I thought."

"Maybe to the others in the *familiya*, but not me." She squirmed and moaned. Her excitement was still palpable.

A hard thrust upwards sent her high into the air, a look of such lust on her face it rocked him. His balls churned, moving in tight to his body. "So, you've noticed how I look at Jal."

"Drool is more like it." Her pussy clenched, sucking at him again in the sexy way she had. "Seen it and thought it was hot."

Brishen gaped, his hips froze. He tried to speak, to ask her what she meant, but nothing came out for a moment. He swallowed and tried again. "Hot? You think it's hot?"

It was her turn to chuckle. Finally she replied, "Yes, very hot. Two studs together. What's not sexy about that?" She leaned up and pressed her lips to his.

The thought of her feeling that way made Brishen's blood boil. He'd never dreamed he'd find a woman who would, or could, accept his feelings for Jal. Hell, he wasn't even sure he accepted them himself.

"Can we stop this yakking? I really need to get fucked." Her voice was stern, yet behind the demand lay a hint of humour.

"I'll do my best." Brishen's tone was nowhere near as steady as hers, but his heart was lighter than it had been in days. "Top or bottom?" He reached around her and took firm hold.

"Bottom." Her arms went around his neck, her legs around his waist, ankles crossed behind him.

Brishen turned them both so he wound up on top, she beneath him, her hair fanned out in the grass. "You just want me to have sore knees," he chided her.

"Better you than me, sexy stud."

He backed out of her, barely leaving just the tip of his cock touching her labia. He moved his legs, and it took but a moment to be ready for her hands on his hips. The firm grip made him shudder. *If only...Jal.* He pushed that thought aside and thrust forward, burying himself to the hilt. The grip she had on him was nearly tight enough. He pulled back, tormenting her with his slow pace and tantalising her with just the tip of his cock against her cunt. He shifted his hips, working them so his shaft slid up and down her groove a dozen times before her frustrated groan made him sink in again. Her legs squeezed him and he growled with pleasure. "Yes, fuck yes."

"Harder, faster, you're killing me," she countered, thrusting herself up against him.

Brishen repositioned himself, easing his knees wider apart and taking her wrists in hand. Holding them, he pulled them high over her head and pressed them into the soft grass. "You want it fast," he teased, leaning forward and kissing her along her neck. "But, what if I want it to last and last?"

"I'll die of frustration!" She twisted her head away and thrust her hips up then slammed down to the ground.

"Can't have that, can I?" He worked his body around then withdrew and took a deep breath, preparing himself for the next few minutes. He knew he'd come. His excitement soared and threatened to overcome him. Even though he couldn't get Jal from his thoughts, this woman, this lush, full-bodied wench, was causing more excitement in him than he'd any right to expect.

He slammed forward, his cock head touching something deep in her body. The suddenness of it thrilled him. Her reaction tortured him. She clamped her cunt down hard, gripping his shaft like a vice.

"Fuck yeah, like that," she murmured and wrapped her calves around his thighs, her arms around his neck. She writhed beneath him as he eased in and out of her sopping wetness. A slick sheen of sweat soon covered them both, and their bodies slipped against each other, adding to the eroticism.

"Hold tight, Tawnie," he murmured and increased the speed of his thrusting. Hard, fast jabs seemed to send her into shuddering bouts of ecstasy. He slammed into her, his belly meeting hers with resounding slaps echoing through the nearby trees.

His balls pulled up, and he knew he'd lose it soon. He gazed down at her, her closed eyes and gaping mouth more attractive than anything he could remember seeing. Her body tensed, her cunt clenched, and she cried out as her climax struck. She milked him, and in only a couple of thrusts, he, too, lost the battle and growled his release. He thrust again, and stars exploded as heat gushed from him.

Her fingers tightened on his shoulders, the nails digging into the flesh. Pain became pleasure as his climax tore through him.

Finally, the stars faded, and he caught his breath. Tawnie inhaled and relaxed her hands. A shudder gripped her, but only for a moment or so. Her face, flushed from pleasure, glowed. Her smile gladdened his heart.

She's not Jal, but she's definitely amazing. Leaning down, he kissed her, sucking at her tongue while she stroked his arms.

When they separated, she gazed up into his eyes. "Thank you, I needed that."

He grinned and made his cock lurch inside her. "I did, too. You're fantastic."

"But not Jal, I know."

"No, not Jal, but fantastic in your own right." His thoughts went back to his father. She was what he'd wanted for him, and Brishen couldn't help but agree. He pushed the image of the dark-skinned Jal aside and bent to kiss Tawnie again.

Chapter Six

Aric walked a few paces ahead of Kai in their normal formation. Even though they were lovers and soul mates, Aric would always be his leader's protector. He moved forward cautiously, nose to the ground, black-tipped tail held straight behind him.

The cougars entered the abandoned old town, *the ghost town*, as most of the changelings in the surrounding territories referred to it. The ruins were ancient and ramshackle. Most of the buildings had fallen into piles of aged timber and broken glass. A store and a barn were the only two structures still recognisable. Tall grass and trees were the most prominent features of the town, now.

Satisfied there were no surprises ahead, Aric breathed easily as they trudged through the brush. The cave where the amulets had been discovered was just on the edge of town. He and Kai had the shortest trip, and he assumed they'd arrive before the others but didn't know for sure.

At the mouth of the cave, he paused and looked back at Kai. *'I'll go in first.'*

His lover nodded.

He proceeded inside, nosing around each familiar nook and cranny until he was certain the cave was empty. The fire pit in the centre of the space was cold. Assorted pelts, scattered on the floor, seemed untouched since the last time he and the kits had been there.

He returned to Kai's side and nuzzled the black fur on his partner's neck. *'It's secure.'*

Kai mimicked the gesture, rubbing the back of one ear along Aric's side. *'And secluded, my golden stud.'*

Aric turned his back to his lover, crouched down low and raised his arse. He wasn't adverse to a little play before the business of work began. Looking over his shoulder, he swished his tail playfully.

With a soft purr, Kai pressed his nose against the proffered opening, his rough tongue licking the puckered hole.

Thrilling sensations rippled through Aric. His cock pulsed, the shaft moving up in its pouch. Before he could respond, the delicious treatment ended.

Kai moved away slowly, regret brimming in his eyes when he caught the gaze of his lover. *'We've much to do before the others arrive. Hopefully, there'll be time for this later.'*

'We'll make time.' Aric butted his head against Kai's shoulder then stepped back. They made eye contact and shrugged off their packs, each beginning the transformation which would return them to human form.

A groan escaped Aric as his bones shifted and his spine realigned. Muscle and sinew elongated so his limbs could stretch into the taller, bulkier shape of a man. Torment, tinged with sweet pleasure, took hold as his body changed. Cool air tickled his smooth, bare skin as his pelt morphed. Rising to his feet, he stretched and luxuriated in each movement. Being a cat was his first love, but becoming a strong man capable of fine dexterity held a thrill of its own.

Kai rummaged through his knapsack and brought out a jerkin and pants. He tossed a lustful glance at Aric's thick, erect cock and muttered, "Get dressed. I can't concentrate with you like that."

With a chuckle, Aric did as advised. He donned clothes similar to Kai's, but unlike his leader, he pulled his long hair back away from his face and tied it with a strip of leather. Kai preferred to let his brown tresses fall around his shoulders. Aric loved that about him and, as he watched the man move around the cave, thought again about jumping his bones. *Later.*

"We'll need a fire," Kai announced. "We'll eat some of the provisions we brought tonight, but we might have to hunt tomorrow."

"Yes. I'll plan to—" Aric heard movement outside and stopped to listen. "Someone's here."

Kai's eyes narrowed. "One of our party, already?" He fingered the gold amulet around his neck. "I don't sense any danger."

"Just to be safe..." Aric pulled a skinning knife from his pack and approached the mouth of the cave. He glanced around warily before spotting the big, black man with the shiny, bald head. Relief coursed through him, and he smiled. "It's a good thing we didn't take our play any further. Our bear friends have arrived."

Tarek's teeth gleamed pearly white when he spotted Aric. "Good day," he called, shouldering a pack as he came forward. Handsome, dark-haired Raven was at his side, both men clothed in garments similar to their own.

Kai stepped shoulder to shoulder with Aric, and they watched the others approach. "Ah yes, Tarek."

"Along with his partner, Raven," Aric informed him. He left the cave and nodded at the bruin leader with the sparkling blue amulet around his neck. "Welcome, Tarek. Hello, Raven. Did Inuka make the trek with you?"

"No." Tarek replied. "I thought it best to leave him behind with the clan. We've had a rash of eager, inexperienced hunters from Newburgen nosing around the territory, lately. Most of them seem to think a bear head would be a fine thing to mount on the wall above their mantles."

"Fools." Kai placed a hand on Tarek's shoulder. "It's good to see you again, old friend."

Tarek grinned. "And you. Kai, this is my partner, Raven."

"Welcome." Kai acknowledged Raven then turned to Tarek. "I was sorry to hear about Skye."

A glimmer of pain crossed Tarek's face, and the smile slipped away. "An unfortunate accident. Time has helped." He cast an adoring glance at Raven. "And the support of close friends."

"Good." Kai stepped aside and motioned towards the cave with a hand. "Come in and take a seat. You've journeyed a good part of the day."

Tarek entered the cave, Raven at his heels. "Not a bad trek. I wouldn't have missed it, to hear more about this new talisman you've found. A horse amulet. Wonders never cease."

Kai followed them in. "Would you like to see it?" He went to his knapsack and retrieved the small pouch. He removed the talisman and glanced at it before passing it to Tarek.

Aric watched the big man examine the amulet with reverence. Kai had polished the purple stone until it shone brilliantly and placed it on a sturdy leather thong. It was a thing of beauty and, at the same time, a mystery.

"It's a stallion, indeed," Tarek said with a touch of wonder. "I've never seen any horse changelings. Raven said he'd heard the wolves had encountered some."

"We're hoping Cole and Zane can shed more light on their whereabouts. Kai has a vague idea where the horses might have settled, but it's a big country and, without knowing for sure, we could take years to find them." Aric paused and listened. Someone else approached, and instinct told him it was the wolves. "Speaking of which…"

The other three men turned towards the cave entrance, their senses also alerted.

"More company," Kai added. "Cole and Zane, I presume?"

Aric and Raven stepped out of the cave to make sure the new arrivals were the expected duo. Aric glanced around, finally spotting the two men making their way through the brush. "Yes, it's them."

"It certainly is," Raven agreed. He glanced up and down Aric's body and added, "You're looking fine and fit today."

"And you're as smooth-talking as ever." Aric focused on the approaching men, trying to ignore the hungry, lust-filled gaze Raven shot at him.

"Still haven't wrapped your mind around a little bi-species fling? I think it's a great idea."

Aric rolled his eyes. He'd have been irritated if he hadn't heard the humour in the dark-haired man's voice. *Raven is jerking my chain.* "I might scratch your eyes out," he countered.

"I'm willing to risk it."

The newcomers were upon them before Aric could respond. He nodded to the two tall men before him. "Cole, Zane, welcome. How was your trip?"

"Not bad." Cole shrugged the pack off his shoulder and grabbed it before it hit the ground. "But I'm ready to sit and take a load off."

"The others are inside." Aric motioned towards the cave. "Come in, join us." He let them walk ahead then followed to make introductions. "Kai, this is Cole, talisman holder of the wolf clan."

Kai stepped forward to greet the man who stood half a head taller than his own imposing stature. "Cole, thank you for coming."

Cole nodded. "This is my partner, Zane." He looked at Tarek and offered a slight dip of his head. "Greetings, Tarek. I trust things are well in bear territory?"

"Better than they were the last time we met." Tarek pointed to the leather thong around Cole's neck and smiled mischievously. "So, it would seem you heeded the call of the talisman. I thought you had some doubts about that. Something about not being ready to settle down."

Cole puffed out his chest. "I didn't 'settle' for anything. I've got two amazing partners, two pups and a tribe who are very loyal to me. We're getting along quite nicely in wolf territory, thank you. Life is good."

"Indeed," Kai agreed, and the three talisman bearers stood in a small circle, each apparently deep in his own private thoughts.

Off to the side, Aric watched them with a feeling of awe in his gut. According to Kai, the three leaders had never been in one spot before, let alone standing so near to each other. Each of them was handsome and virile and bore a great responsibility. He studied their differences. Kai, with his long, flowing hair and muscular physique Aric found perfect in every way. Tarek, dark skinned and with a totally hairless head, stood about the same height but was broader through the chest. Cole, the tallest of the three, was also the leanest, though he appeared to have muscles in all the right places. He also seemed to be the youngest and, judging by the way he carried himself, possibly the one who felt like he had something to prove.

Kai took a step back and looked at the other two leaders. "Again, I thank you for coming. I could have sought out the horses on my own but felt it prudent to keep all of the tribes informed. We changelings share a kinship that should never be broken. Time has proven that we're stronger standing together when facing adversity. If we're to accept another tribe into our brotherhood, I want everyone to know about it so there are no surprises."

Cole faced him. "So there's truly a fourth amulet?"

Tarek held up the leather strap and let the shimmering stone dangle in front of Cole's face.

"Horses," Cole murmured under his breath, his gaze on the talisman. "No doubt about it."

Kai cast an annoyed glance at him and replied, "Did you think I brought you here under false pretences? Of course there's another amulet. I was given to believe you might have seen some wild stallions, changelings, like us. Or was the story you told my emissary merely a ploy to bolster yourself in our eyes?"

Amused at the exchange, Aric bit back a chuckle. Kai had little patience for anyone questioning him and obviously intended to put the younger tribal leader in his place right then.

Cole apparently realised his mistake and took a step back, bowing his head. "I meant no disrespect, Kai. The discovery of the fourth talisman was quite a surprise. It's been a long day's journey, and I was anxious to get to the reason for our trip."

As if the episode were already forgotten, Kai smiled and nodded. He spread his hands, palms open. "Please, everyone. Have a seat. I thought we'd dine on the provisions we brought and, since everyone is here, we might as well get down to business."

Raven lifted his pack. "We'll share our foodstuffs, as well."

From his knapsack, Zane pulled a bottle and smiled. "We brought dandelion wine, brewed by our Uncle Kaleb, one of the elders in our tribe. It's got a nice punch to it."

Aric gazed upon the bottle sceptically. "Alcohol makes men stupid. People from Newburgen have proved that fact to us, time and again."

Cole shook his head. "The hunters we encounter don't need liquid assistance to foster their ignorance. They seem to have that quality ingrained in them." He smiled and pulled a similar bottle from his pack. "There are six of us, and only three bottles of wine. Surely not enough to make anyone here too stupid."

Tarek's hearty laughter rumbled throughout the cave and seemed to put everyone at ease. Before long, they were all lounging on pelts in front of the fire, eating jerky and fruit and passing around the wine, which Aric found tasted surprisingly good.

"We spotted the horses at the northern edge of our territory, where the river forms a waterfall going over a cliff." Cole took a swig then went on. "There were two of them the first time. Large, handsome stallions. They appeared healthy and well fed. Not like the strays that occasionally wander away from town."

Zane nodded. "The second time we saw them, there were four or five together, and at least one was a mare. So wherever they are, I suspect there'll be more."

Leaning back on one elbow, Raven gnawed on a piece of jerky and spoke between bites. "I know that waterfall. We can make it there in a day. Finding the horse camp might take longer, but if we all spread out—"

Kai shook his head. "I didn't intend for everyone to make the trip. Aric and I will go, of course."

Shrugging, Cole looked at him. "It's very close to where we live. We might as well go with you."

Tarek raised a bottle to his lips and polished off the last few drops of its contents. He wiped his mouth with the back of his hand and grinned. "We didn't come all this way to be left behind. So it's settled, then."

Intrigued, Aric watched Kai take a deep breath while glancing around the room. Kai had very little choice but to accept the offers from the other tribes lest he look ungrateful. Aric knew Kai was concerned that a large group could overwhelm the changelings, who might think they were the only shifters around

Kai finally nodded in acceptance. "We'll go together, but when we reach their territory, we must tread lightly. We can't be sure how much these animals know."

Tarek widened his eyes and said with mock horror, "You mean, they might be shocked to see bears, cougars and wolves at their doorstep, all wearing little backpacks?"

Chuckles filtered through the group. Kai rolled his eyes. "I don't intend to face these creatures as a cougar. Communication would be extremely difficult. We'll shift to human form when we get close. And we'll need clothes. Hence, the 'little backpacks'."

Once again, Tarek opened his mouth to say something, but Kai cut him off. "I know, Tarek. You'd be quite happy if six naked men arrived at your camp, but we're going to use a little propriety."

The bear leader's booming laughter echoed throughout the cave. "Propriety? What the fuck is that?" He looked around and added, "Did someone say there was another bottle of wine?"

* * * *

The six men stayed awake well into the night, talking and polishing off the rest of the homebrewed beverage. When morning came, they ate another meal, packed up their belongings and shifted to their animal forms. Aric figured they must make quite a sight, two nimble wolves followed by two large black bears then the sleek cougars bringing up the rear. They travelled at a brisk pace until

Tarek stopped, seemingly without reason. The others glanced around, but Aric spotted nothing amiss. Suddenly, Tarek transformed into the guise of a man.

Tarek took a moment to gather himself then turned to Kai. "There's something wrong with my tribe." He fingered the amulet around his neck.

The blue stone glowed. Aric glanced at it then back at Kai.

Raven reared up on his back legs and growled.

"Yes, we'll leave for home immediately," Tarek assured him.

Fur on the back of his neck bristling, Kai looked at Tarek and nodded towards the group.

Aric wondered if his lover would shift to converse with the others, but he seemed to get his meaning across without words.

Eyes shining with concern, Tarek smiled gently and laid a hand on Kai's shoulder. "Thank you, old friend, but we'll be fine. You four continue your journey. Perhaps you could stop by on your way back and let us know what happened."

Kai nodded, and reared up to raise a paw to Tarek's shoulder. *'Good luck, my friend.'*

Aric heard the words in his partner's head, though he was sure no one else could.

Tarek seemed to understand. He nodded at Kai again then stepped back, transforming into a bear. With a mighty leap, he took off in the direction of home at incredible speed, Raven at his heels.

Aric and Kai exchanged glances. *'They'll be fine,'* Kai told him mentally. *'I sense a problem, but nothing Tarek can't handle.'*

Aric nodded.

'We need to keep moving.' Kai hurried to join Cole and Zane, who waited for them. The three headed down their original path, and Aric jogged to catch up.

The terrain slowly changed. Formerly passing through tree-lined meadows, they were now entering the foothills of a good sized mountain range that required more climbing than walking. When they reached a plateau with a nice, shady spot by the river, Aric was glad to stop for a drink and a breather. He stood at the edge of the water and lapped it up greedily then found a spot in the grass and flopped down.

Kai stretched out next to him.

When the wolves had drunk their fill, they slunk to the grass and both collapsed. Cole looked at Aric and nodded in the direction of a pass leading through the mountains.

'The wolf dens are that way,' Aric conveyed to Kai.

'Any idea where they saw the horses?' Kai wondered.

Aric sat up and glanced around.

Cole seemed to understand. He stood and headed away from the direction of his home, pausing to look back to see if they were following.

'It would seem he's ready to go.' Aric's mouth gaped open as a huge yawn escaped.

'Come on.' Kai stood and butted his head against his lover's shoulder. He fell in behind the wolfen leader, and the other two came along behind.

They hadn't travelled far when Cole froze, his tail held low behind him.

Aric searched for whatever Cole had spotted, and his heart lurched. Two handsome stallions eating grass not a stone's throw from where they stood. He turned to Kai, and they shared a glance.

'Can it be this easy?' Aric marvelled.

'We can only hope. Let's watch them for a while before we shift. We don't know how far they are from wherever it is they call home.'

Quietly, Kai and Aric made sure they weren't downwind, then settled into the grass to keep out of sight.

Cole and Zane followed their lead and did the same.

Kai glanced at Aric. *'Now, we wait.'*

Excitement tightened Aric's gut. They were on the verge of something amazing, he felt it. Placing a talisman in the hands of a tribe who'd never had one before. *Amazing might be an understatement.* He kept his eyes on the stallions and waited.

Chapter Seven

Brishen sidled towards Jal, unsure of himself but determined to finally come to terms with the feelings he had. His heart fluttered. Even thinking about how close he could get to the man, the beast, made him shiver with pleasure. He whinnied, and Jal raised his head. Nose to nose, they stood together, each inhaling the other's breath.

Finally, Brishen couldn't stand doing nothing for a moment longer. He stepped forward and ran his chin along Jal's back. Another step brought his muzzle level with the horse's flank, and he nudged the muscular hind end.

Jal danced to the side and looked at him.

Brishen's cock swelled, the tip emerging from the sheath. He shuddered, dropped to his knees and changed. Pain flashed through him as his bones shifted. Agony turned to ecstasy as his body realigned, the coat of hair morphing into flesh, his elongated muzzle condensing into the face of a man.

Beside him, Jal did the same. A grunt, followed by a long sigh, bespoke the pain-pleasure of the transformation. The man lowered to the ground and arched his body. Arms and legs emerged. Hands and feet took on human form.

Brishen's gaze lowered to the man's middle. A washboard-rippled belly gave way to the smoothness of groin. Pubic hair curled around the base of an impressive cock. Balls, sparsely haired, lay nestled between his granite-strong thighs. Mouth watering, Brishen pulled himself a little closer.

"What's the matter?" Jal rolled to his side, facing Brishen. He reached out and slid his hand over Brishen's arm. "What's going on in that head of yours?"

Brishen bit back the rush of words threatening to explode from him. He gathered his thoughts before again turning to face the man who set his world on end. "I care for you."

Jal cocked his head and smiled. "Yes, I know. It took you long enough to realise it." His hand wandered to Brishen's chest, centring on a nipple. Tweaking it made Brishen gasp.

"But, I care for you in a way I'm not sure about." This wasn't coming out as Brishen had hoped. He took a deep breath and tried again. "I want you."

A smile curled Jal's lips upwards. "You want me." He chuckled then added, "Well, it's about bloody time."

It was Brishen's turn to smile, then his face grew warm. "I've never…"

"I know, but it's all right," Jal whispered and reached for him. His hand wound around Brishen's neck and drew him forward.

Brishen couldn't take his eyes off Jal's dark brown orbs. Their lips brushed, and a soft groan escaped him. His tongue flicked out, dabbing at Jal's mouth, tasting the salty sweat of his upper lip.

"Come here, you sexy beast," Jal murmured and, slipping his arm more firmly around Brishen, drew him on top.

Brishen straddled Jal's hips, his knees on the rough ground on either side, his hands bracketing his head. Naked, their erections rubbed and dragged against each other, sending jolts of excitement through Brishen like he'd never felt before. The slick pre-cum leaking from his own cock joined with Jal's and made an amazing lubricant.

What am I doing? His mind reeled, thoughts racing in a dozen different directions, yet it felt so right. *My father.*

Jal cupped Brishen's buttocks and drew him even more firmly against the rampaging shaft Brishen wanted suddenly to suck and nuzzle. Their lips touched, pressed hungrily together, even as Brishen's thoughts sank into the realm of eroticism he'd scarcely dared dream about. Sweat formed on his brow and under his arms. He clenched his arse cheeks and shivered, his desires darting to the deeper fantasy of being penetrated.

When his breath was spent, he broke their kiss and sat up just enough to allow his hand free rein between them. He reached down and slid his fingers beneath the shaft of Jal's cock. Warm and firm, familiar, yet so different from his own. Smooth flesh covered the length, the vein, running slightly more to the centre of the shaft, pulsed against his fingers.

"Yeah, do me, stroke me, please, my sexy man," Jal murmured and thrust his hips up, lifting both himself and Brishen.

Brishen's knee slipped to the side, stopping only when it collided with a stone and sent a stab of pain up his leg. He grunted but soon forgot the minor injury when Jal cupped a hand around Brishen's rod. They toyed and teased each other, learning what turned on their new lover while firing the excitement, making their breaths come in short gasps.

Pre-cum oozed from them both, creating the slickest of avenues for them to play in. When Brishen clenched Jal's bum and thrust into Jal's fist repeatedly, he knew it was time to stop. He released Jal's cock and rolled to the side. He wound up on his knees and faced away from Jal, his arse perfectly presented.

"Oh yeah, that's what I'm after." Jal climbed to his knees and positioned himself to Brishen's rear. "Put your head down." He gripped Brishen's buttocks, one in each hand, and pried them apart. "Cross your arms under your head."

Brishen did as Jal asked and soon found himself in the most exposed position he could imagine. When Jal kneed his thighs apart, forcing him to spread his legs even wider, he realised just how much more revealed he was.

"The thing you have to remember, here, is to relax." Jal's fingers worked towards the crinkled flesh around Brishen's anus, pressing and stroking him there. "Don't tense up and don't try to keep me from spreading you wide."

"You've done this before?" Brishen asked, gazing over his shoulder at the man whose attention was completely focussed on his arse.

"Yes, and I know what feels good and what doesn't. You tense up, and it will hurt." Jal glanced away from Brishen's bottom and looked him in the eye as if to make sure he understood. "I wouldn't hurt you for the world. I..." He stopped and returned his gaze to Brishen's bum. "I care too much to hurt you."

Brishen shifted, getting as comfortable as he possibly could and sighed. With his eyes closed and his cheek resting on his forearm, he was in near bliss. He was about to reply to Jal's last comment when the slickest, wettest, most amazing sensation slid over his anus.

He clenched but instantly relaxed when he realised it was Jal's tongue wetting his pucker. Shuddering, he whispered, "That's amazing."

Jal pressed the tip against the opening, wiggling it until Brishen felt it enter. Smooth, wet and like nothing else in the world, the man's tongue eased in deeper. When lips pressed against his flesh and the bristles of Jal's beard brushed against his cheeks, Brishen thought he'd go mad with lust. His cock pulsed and slapped his belly in response. Jal fucked him with the long tongue then used his fingers to loosen the muscles surrounding Brishen's hole. A slight pressure against his pucker quickly became the sensation of fullness as one finger entered him. Saliva eased the way, and the finger's teasing wiggles soon had him pushing back, wanting more. And more came, another finger sliding alongside the first. Two digits tormented him, drove him to heights of pleasure he'd only dreamed of.

Stars flashed behind his eyes. He reached beneath himself for the shaft of his cock and masturbated it, slowly, unwilling to bring the episode to an end.

Jal shifted, moving his lips and tongue to the back of Brishen's balls. He sucked at them, slathering his tongue over the crinkled flesh.

"Jal, I can't stand it any more," Brishen muttered. His body moved against his lover's mouth and fingers. The excitement mounted.

Jal backed away, his fingers still worming in and out of Brishen's arse. "Tell me what you want. I'll do anything, just tell me."

Brishen rose onto his hands and knees, relinquishing his hold on his cock. It dangled, pulsing with need. He looked over his shoulder and gasped. Jal's face was flushed, his chest heaving. But what really drew his attention was the man's cock. Fully erect, it pointed his way, the head as large as a plum.

"Fuck me. I need you inside me. Please, fuck me with that monster cock of yours."

"Only if you're sure." Jal's tone was uncertain.

That surprised Brishen.

"I'll need to stretch you some more." Jal slipped yet one more finger into Brishen's hole, working them from side to side, stretching the delicate tissue.

"Ugh, yeah. Oh my, fucking hell." Brishen's mind was mush. He couldn't think straight. His focus zeroed in on his genitals. His cock ached, and his balls were on fire. Yet it was his hole, and the treatment it was receiving, that took his breath.

"Yeah, like that," Jal crooned while working his fingers in and out, spreading them a little more each time.

Brishen rocked on the man's hand. His arse was hungry for the teasing, even hungrier for the waiting cock. When he couldn't take it any longer, he growled and said, "Now, I need it now. Fuck me, Jal."

He felt rather than saw Jal move into position. The man pulled his fingers free, slowly, carefully, then a warm, wet presence nudged his hole. The dome of Jal's cock pressed against the loosened muscle and popped inside.

A slight pain knifed into Brishen's gut, but only for an instant. Jal remained still until Brishen pushed back.

"Oh fuck, oh fuck." Brishen sank onto Jal's erection. The sensation of being filled was unbelievable. The stretching thrilled him. The man's cock pulsed, and he felt it. He shifted, and his breath exploded from him. He couldn't gasp for air. He couldn't see or move.

Jal's hands on his hips held him in place while the man sank in fully. When Jal's balls pressed against the back of Brishen's sac, both men sighed. They were still, the only movement the rise and fall of their chests.

When Brishen's bum clenched, he shivered. A new, delicious torment rippled from his backside, radiating into his thighs, his belly, even up his back.

He clenched again, determined to wring every bit of feeling from his first fucking as he could. *I love this.*

Jal groaned and made his cock pulse.

"Oh fuck!" Brishen murmured.

"You ready?" Jal asked in a concerned tone.

"Yeah, slow and easy."

"All right. Take a deep breath." Jal's grip on Brishen's haunch tightened, then he slowly pulled his cock nearly all the way out.

It felt as if Brishen's insides were being yanked out of his arse, yet there was no pain or discomfort. In fact, it was amazing. Exciting…transforming…thrilling… He couldn't find the right words, but he knew he loved it. When Jal stopped with just the tip resting against his outer pucker,

Brishen nearly screamed for him not to go any farther. He couldn't bear the thought of the man's cock leaving him.

"Steady," Jal whispered and stroked Brishen's back. "Trust me. You'll enjoy this."

Brishen calmed his thoughts and waited for Jal to continue. It wasn't a long wait. Within moments, the handsome stud leaned in, sending his thick cock back into the depths of Brishen's hole. Again, Jal paused, but only for the barest instant before withdrawing to the outer ring.

"Yesss," Brishen groaned as Jal entered him then retreated. His insides grew accustomed to the movements, his anal muscles clenched on Jal's shaft, gripping and tugging at the monster invading him. His own erection had shrunk a little at the initial insertion of Jal into his hole, but as the pleasure had grown, so had his cock.

"Ready for more?" Jal asked when they'd been seesawing for blissful seconds.

Sweat streamed off him, yet Brishen was eager for the exercise to come. He took hold of his stiffened shaft. "Yeah, do me. Fuck me hard." He braced himself for the onslaught and smiled when Jal's grip tightened even more on his hips. The fucking took on a forceful tone, their guttural groans of pleasure becoming louder, filling the sunlit mountainside with their sounds of bliss.

"More, more," Brishen growled and slammed back his arse. The slapping of flesh on flesh became their music, their sobs of pleasure, the words. "Faster, harder."

"I'm close, I'm going to come." Jal ground his hips against Brishen's bottom then pulled out and slammed back in. Twice more he lunged into Brishen before the dance was done and cum filled Brishen's hole in spasmodic spurts.

"Yes, yes, fill me up, my sexy stud." Brishen gripped his cock tightly, not willing to shoot his own load quite yet. He churned his arse, trying to milk the last drop from his lover.

Jal exhaled explosively before collapsing across Brishen's back. Sated, the man seemed quite happy to simply lie there and gasp. Eventually, he slipped his fingers around Brishen's shaft and stroked him. "You're still hard. Did I not pleasure you enough?"

"Yes, you gave me incredible pleasure," Brishen replied, turning to kiss the side of Jal's face. "But, I want to feel your mouth on me. It's one of my biggest fantasies."

"Ah, I see." Jal rose from Brishen's back and carefully pulled free of his bum.

The feeling of emptiness was surprising to Brishen.

"And one I share with you. I've wanted to taste you for nearly as long as I've known you."

"And I've been too worried about what my father expected of me to see." Brishen silently chastised himself as a fool, even as Jal coaxed him onto his back. It didn't take much urging. A gentle push, and Brishen rolled over. The ground wasn't exactly soft, but he'd found a spot where the rocks had been buried beneath a covering of grass. He wriggled and spread his legs.

"True, but we're here now," Jal replied, eying Brishen's erection lying across his lower belly. "And I'm starving."

Brishen slid his hands under his head and made himself look as appetising as possible. "Well, if you're that hungry, I'm definitely ready to fill your belly."

Without any further encouragement, Jal lay between Brishen's legs. He slipped one arm under each thigh and pulled, bringing himself to the meal he seemed so eager to dine on. A moment later, Brishen had to bite back a groan as the man's mouth took both of his balls and drew them in. Warm suction made his head spin. The heat was enough to make his sac shift and pull up. Yet, the mouth refused to let them. Brishen was in a sea of bliss. His hips thrust upward, unbidden, nearly pulling the orbs from Jal's mouth.

"I need you on my cock. I'm going crazy here." Brishen couldn't keep the demanding tone from his voice.

Jal seemed to like it and, an instant later, wrapped his lips around the head while his fingers caressed Brishen's aching balls.

Myriad sensations tore at Brishen. Pleasure beyond his wildest dreams enveloped him. He stroked Jal's hair, his face, and gasped when the man deep-throated his throbbing cock to the base.

"Take it, take it all," crooned Brishen as he humped the man's face. His grip shifted to Jal's ears, and he used them like handles, dragging him down then shoving him away. The speed increased, and Brishen was sure Jal struggled to catch his breath, but for the moment, it didn't matter. He needed to come, and Jal seemed as determined as he was to make that happen.

The shaft of Brishen's cock pulsed hard. He was ready. There was no turning back. He growled and dragged Jal's mouth down until the man's lips met the flesh of his groin. Jal swallowed, the muscles in his throat milking Brishen ruthlessly.

"Yeah, fuck...oh yeah!" The words exploded from Brishen just as cum gushed from his cock. An enormous grunt came from deep inside him, then another pulse sent the next gushing mouthful into Jal's gullet. Three more times, Brishen shuddered and sent geysers of cream into the man's mouth, and each time Jal swallowed it as if relishing the tasty treat.

When his orgasm faded, Brishen relaxed the grip he'd had on Jal's ears and smiled when the man pulled off his cock.

"Damn, you've about drowned me, Brishen."

"I couldn't take the chance of you going hungry." Brishen held out his arms, needing to hold the man who'd opened an entire new world to him. His heart came near to bursting at that moment, and he realised that no matter what, he loved Jal.

"Thank you," Jal said, snuggling against Brishen's chest.

Brishen looked down, trying to see into Jal's eyes. "Why are you thanking me? It's I who should be grateful to you. You've been so damn patient with me, you deserve a medal."

Jal tilted up his face, smiling at his lover. "Yes, maybe. But, you finally let me love you." He bent down and kissed Brishen on the chest. "I know your father was adamant that you have a wife, but maybe you can have both. Me to love you, and a wife to bear your young."

A rustling in the brush across the clearing made Brishen look away from his lover's face. The trees were thick on that side, and he saw nothing, at first. Then, a shadow moved.

He pushed free of Jal and leapt to his feet, staring into the underbrush. Shapes moved, yet he felt no threat. *What is going on?*

Jal stood and came to stand beside him. "What's the matter, Brishen?"

"I'm not sure. I thought I saw movement."

Something rustled again, and when two familiar figures stepped forward, Brishen relaxed. Niron and Buc, two members of his gypsy *familya*, distant cousins, appeared excited to see him.

"Brishen!" Buc's eyes lit up. "We've been looking for you. There are men in our camp."

Uneasiness niggled at Brishen again. "What do you mean, men? Hunters from Newburgen? Do they carry weapons?"

"They don't have guns." Buc shook his head. "They really don't look like hunters. But there are four of them, and they asked to speak with our leader. Our *tribal leader* was how the one guy put it."

"'Tribal leader'," Brishen repeated. Thoughts raced through his mind. *What men would use the words 'tribal leader', unless they were of a tribe, themselves?*

A thoughtful expression crossed Niron's face. "It was strange, Brishen. They didn't seem surprised when they wandered into our camp. Usually when people from town stumble upon us, they get all nervous and weird. You know what I mean."

"I know." Brishen definitely understood the reaction Niron spoke of. People didn't seem to care much for gypsies, especially a band that was even more unusual than most. No one knew their changeling secret, of course, but others apparently sensed something out of the ordinary. On the rare occasions when Brishen had joined his father on visits to town or had any dealings with the townsfolk, the people had seemed uncomfortable around them. The gypsies had been encouraged to hurry about their business and be off.

"These men are different," Buc concluded.

Niron nodded.

"I guess we should go see what this is all about." Brishen glanced at Jal. "Come with me?"

"Of course."

"Let's go in through the back way and grab some clothes before we meet our guests." He turned to his cousins. "Tell the strangers I'll meet with them shortly. Offer them refreshments."

Buc rolled his eyes. "The women have taken care of that." He added conspiratorially, "These fellows aren't hard to look at. The females are practically crawling over them."

With a scowl on his face, Brishen headed for the path which provided another entrance to camp. "Then go rescue the poor guys or something," he called over his shoulder. "We'll be right there."

He nodded to Jal, and they proceeded quickly to the large circle of tents and wagons. They reached Jal's tent first and stopped to dress. After donning one of his lover's cotton shirt and trousers, Brishen slipped into a pair of work boots and laced them up. He stood and checked his appearance. "Thanks." He smiled at Jal. "You're just my size."

Jal leaned in, his mouth next to Brishen's ear. "I think we discovered that earlier today." He kissed the lobe and took a step back.

Despite their pressing business, Brishen took a moment to let the warm feelings from their encounter flow through him. He gazed into the eyes of the man he was quickly growing to adore. There was so much he wanted to say, but this wasn't the time. He glanced through the tent flap towards the centre of camp then returned his focus to Jal.

"You'll back me up, here? I'm not exactly sure what we're getting into."

"I'm here for you, always. Be strong, my love. Let these people know who they're dealing with. Brishen, King of the Gypsies."

The words were like arrows of excitement through Brishen's heart. Out of respect for his father, there hadn't been a crowning ceremony, yet. But after the proper amount of mourning time, the rite would mark what everyone already expected and knew. *I will be King.*

He inhaled a calming breath and blew it out. "Shall we go?"

Jal's breath warmed the back of his neck. "One step behind you, Sire."

Brishen froze. He understood the formalities and the title afforded kings, but to have that attention directed at him caused a feeling of exhilaration beyond compare. *It's a day for new and exciting things,* he decided. So far, everything had been good. He fervently hoped the trend continued.

A fire blazed in the pit at the centre of the camp. Four men sat on the old chairs and boxes the *familya* had scattered there. They conversed in a pleasant manner with the tribe members, while several females stood back, gaping and chatting about the newcomers.

For a moment, Brishen wondered if Tawnie was among them. He stole a quick glance and was pleased to see she wasn't. Attention back to the matter at hand, he took a deep breath, stood tall and approached the group. "Someone wanted to speak to me?"

All eyes were instantly upon him. Brishen's gaze went from the thinnest man with long, almost white hair to the similarly thin, dark-haired fellow next to him. The third man was more muscular, his blond hair pulled away from his face. But it was the final stranger who captured Brishen's interest. Broad-chested and obviously very strong, the man had dark hair flowing around his shoulders like a mane. There was something virile and civilised about him, yet Brishen sensed a feral side to him, just below the surface.

The man stood and smiled. He motioned to each of the others as he spoke. "Thank you for seeing us. I'd like to introduce my partner Aric, and our friends Cole and Zane." He paused. "I'm Kai, and I have a matter of great importance to bring to you."

Brishen's heart nearly leapt from his chest. *Kai? From my father's dream?* The moment was surreal, and for an instant, he wondered if *he* was dreaming. He clenched his fists, digging his nails into his palms. The pain helped him focus and realise he was *not* dreaming.

He nodded at Kai, whom he now knew to be a cougar changeling. It made perfect sense. He could easily visualise the man shifting into a cat. "I was told to expect you. I am Brishen, son of Shandor. My father was the King of the Gypsies."

"Was?" Kai asked gently.

"He recently passed."

Kai dipped his head reverently. "Our sympathies to you and your people. Not to seem uncaring, but I must ask. Your father's passing makes you the tribal leader?"

Brishen inhaled. He'd discussed this with no one except Jal. It still felt strange and new to him. But it was time to face facts. "Yes. There'll need to be a crowning ceremony, but I'll be the next king."

A smile crept across Kai's face. "Then you're just the man I've been looking for."

Chapter Eight

Aric stretched his legs towards the fire. They'd eaten a meal courtesy of the gypsies, listened to violin music and watched some of them dance until the sun went down. Most of the clan members had come and gone as the night grew dark until finally it was just young, excitable Brishen and his quiet friend Jal sitting near the fire with him and his travelling companions.

Brishen glanced around and apparently noticed the same thing Aric had. The men were alone. "Is it time to get down to business?" the eager, would-be king asked Kai. "I want to know more about why you came."

Kai leant back and casually folded his arms across his chest. "You mentioned you were expecting me. Who spoke my name to you?"

"My father, just before he died. He had a dream about someone named Cato and a cougar-man called Kai who could help the horse-changeling *natsia* reunite. There's been fighting among the *vitsas* for years. *Familyas* travel with caution through the territory lest another *vitsa* ambush and rob them."

To get a better understanding, Aric spoke up so Kai wouldn't have to. "*Familya* is your family group. What's a *vitsa*, a *natsia*?"

With an eager nod, Brishen waved his hands as he spoke. "This is my *familya*, the twenty or so people that live right here. We stay in this part of the territory until the weather grows harsh and we need better shelter. This is closer to water, and we have more room to run, so we stay here as long as we can. Then we head up the mountain and make use of the caves there."

Beside him, Kai nodded. Aric knew the bears lived a similar existence.

"Sometimes people from town discover us and start coming around. When that happens, it's time to go. We move a few miles this way or that, and unless we encroach on another *vitsa*—what you might call a clan—the problems resolve themselves."

"And the *natsia*?" Aric questioned.

"It's the gypsy word for nation." Brishen's eyes looked skyward as if he searched for the proper translation. "It's the whole group of horse changelings. What was that expression you used earlier—tribal leader? We have tribes, too, but they're more like *vitsas*. Small groups of families. The *natsia* is the whole of us."

"Different terminology." Kai raised his hands and shrugged. "I'm the leader of the cougar tribe, which contains various clans. Cole, here, is the wolfen leader. His family groups are called packs. Our third counterpart is a

217

tribe of bears who live in the forest back the way we came from. They also winter in the mountain caves."

"So there are three other *natsias* of changelings—cougars, wolves and bears." Brishen apparently tried to wrap his mind around the new information.

"We *thought* there were three *natsias* of changelings." Kai smiled. "It would seem there are actually four."

The young gypsy leader's eyes grew wide. He turned to his dark-skinned friend and they exchanged glances. Brishen looked back at Kai. "What you say is true, of course. We just thought we were alone, all this time. To find out we're actually a part of something greater is an amazing discovery."

"Excuse me, Brishen." Cole spoke up. "Your father, Shandor, was King of the Gypsies. Did he not rule over the entire *natsia*?"

"In name only. We've been warring for so long, no one paid much attention to an old man with a title. Each *vitsa* has its own leader, a *Bandoleer*. At some point, they became the ones in power. My father's been ill for a long time. His concern was what might happen when word spread of his death."

Kai nodded to Aric. "This sounds much like what Cato went through when the amulets were first discovered. All the changeling nations were in upheaval, and there was great unrest. Cato tackled one tribe at a time, beginning with his own, the cougars. He went from clan to clan, showing them how the amulets could bring peace. He gave them visions of what might happen if the clans didn't come together as one. In just a few generations, the changelings would have died out."

"My father spoke of these amulets and the power they held. At the time, I wondered if his words were the ravings of a dying old man."

Aric watched Kai pull the golden amulet from his shirt and hold it out so all could see. "The amulets are real. The magic they hold is powerful and could be dangerous in the wrong hands."

Cole reached under his tunic and brought out the red amulet for the wide-eyed gypsies' inspection. "I'm not so sure about the danger. The thing won't work for just anybody. There are limits and restrictions. The bearer must be mated for life. He and his mate must have the good of the tribe in their hearts—"

With a reproachful glance, Kai cut him off. "The dangers are very real, my friend. Those who haven't put the talisman to the test are fortunate. It's never wise to toy with something we don't really understand."

Brishen licked his lips, his eyes shining.

His quiet friend, Jal, finally spoke. "I don't understand any of this. What limits? What are the rules? We should know what the necklace *can* do before we can understand what it can't."

Aric bit his lip to keep from chuckling. He wanted to speak but had no doubt Kai would be all over the boy's innocent questions. He knew his lover well.

True to form, Kai's eyes glinted with irritation. He got up and paced around the fire, apparently choosing his words carefully. Eventually he stopped walking and faced Brishen and Jal. Once again, he held out the golden stone, which he wore on a leather thong around his neck, and shook it at them. "The *amulet* is a very powerful talisman. This one increases my senses five-fold. I'm able to sense danger before it happens. You can imagine how those gifts benefit changeling species."

Brishen sprang to his feet. "Remarkable! With those abilities, our lives would be so much easier."

Kai's shoulders sagged. "It's not about making your life *easy*, young one. Your existence should have meaning. Your choices should benefit not only your *familya* but the entire horse *natsia*. Every decision, every mark made, should be done with the good of the earth in mind."

"I'm not that young!" Brishen retorted. "I'm a man. I was raised to adulthood by my father, who taught me all the lessons you're trying to impart. I know very well how our decisions impact Mother Earth. And I know what it means to get along with other people. But I refuse to get pushed around. I was raised a gypsy. We do for ourselves, or we don't do at all. We may not have much, be we'll always have pride."

"And that, young Brishen, may be your downfall." Kai turned and walked away.

"You have a horse amulet?" Brishen shouted after him.

Kai froze, answering without turning around. "I do."

"I want it." Brishen's face flushed red. He crossed his arms over his chest and widened his stance.

Still facing away, Kai replied, "We'll talk about this more tomorrow. It's been a long day. I'd like to get some sleep."

"*Gaje!*" Brishen spat.

Kai turned around slowly and faced him. "Excuse me?"

"*Gaje*. A person who's not a gypsy. You don't understand my path until you've walked in my boots."

"Possibly." Kai nodded once. "But we share another kinship that you've yet to acknowledge. We're both changelings. Part man, part beast. That alone should bind us together.

"I've walked a path similar to yours. Use my experience to help guide your way. I'm offering you counsel. If you're wise, you'll take advantage of it. My guidance, and that of my counterparts, could very well be the thing that makes your life, and that of your *natsia*, easier."

Aric saw Brishen's face grow redder. The boy was obviously young and impetuous, but Aric sensed something greater within him. Brishen had a combination of strength and heart, traits that would serve him well on his journey through life. Kai must have sensed it, too, or he wouldn't be wasting his time. If only they could find a way to harness that energy without breaking the young stallion's spirit.

Brishen clenched his jaw. "I had a father, but he's gone now. I don't need another one. No one asked for your help. Just for the amulet that's rightfully mine."

"Is it?" Kai smiled. "We've yet to discover that. Unfortunately, the determination will have to be saved for another time. As I mentioned, it's been a long day."

Without replying, Brishen turned and went to a nearby tent. He stuck his head in and, in a voice loud enough for them all to hear, said, "Tawnie, could I trouble you to prepare tents for our guests?"

She emerged, fully clothed and wide awake. "It's no trouble, Brishen. We readied the tents earlier. I've just been waiting for you to call me."

He smiled at her, and the pretty, pale-haired woman batted her eyes in return. Aric watched the exchange with amusement. She'd obviously been listening from her tent. Did she have more than a passing interest in Brishen and what the future held for him?

Brishen touched her arm lightly then turned back to the others. "Tawnie will show you your accommodations. I'll see you tomorrow." He didn't wait for a response, just strolled towards the trees. Once he was out of the firelight, he seemed to disappear.

Weariness showed in the shadows that played on Kai's face. "Quick-tempered fellow."

Jal hopped to his feet. "He's a good man."

Tawnie nodded. "You won't find one better."

Kai smiled. "Any man with such loyal friends has to have some redeeming qualities. I'll talk to him again tomorrow. I'm not trying to take the place of his father. I only want him to go into this thing with his eyes, and his heart, wide open."

Tawnie rubbed her hands over her arms. "This *thing* scares me."

With two swift steps, Jal was at her side. "There's no need to be frightened, Tawnie. Please, show our guests to their tents then come back and sit with me by the fire. We'll talk awhile."

She smiled gratefully and motioned for the others to follow her.

Kai did, with Cole and Zane right behind him.

"I'll be along shortly," Aric called. He glanced at Jal, who had taken the seat next to him. "I thought perhaps you and I should talk a bit, first."

Jal looked after Tawnie and the small group of men following her. He nodded and said, "Surely. What's on your mind, Aric?"

"It's not so much what's on my mind as what questions you might have."

"Me? But it's Brishen who leads us."

"True, but I sense a great deal of caring between you and him." Aric leant back and stretched his arms behind his head. It'd been a very long day, and every muscle in his body ached. He looked forward to following Kai. Yet, this young man seemed the ideal person to talk to about this new tribe.

"Yes, of course I care about Brishen. He's going to be crowned our king."

Aric chuckled, but when he saw the fire in Jal's eyes, he bit back his merriment. "I mean no disrespect. He's young, as you are, and he's got a lot of things to learn in a hurry."

Again, Jal seemed eager to defend Brishen. "He'll do just fine. His father taught him well, and he's always known he'd be king one day."

"I got that. But with the amulet, there's more to it now."

Jal appeared to relax, even leaning back and crossing his ankles before going on. "This amulet, Brishen said his father spoke of it. What exactly does it do?"

"Kai told you as much as he can tell anyone. It enhances the bearer's senses to an outstanding degree. He can speak to the clans without really talking. Mind to mind. He sees things before they happen."

"You're serious, aren't you?"

"Yeah. And with it, the holder will have the power to bring your *vitsas* together, all of your clans. Your *natsia* will be strong again."

Jal looked at him for a long moment as if he were either crazy or some kind of fortune teller. Then he looked away and seemed lost in thought. The silence of the night was broken only by the occasional murmur from a tent or wagon. Even the visitors' tent was quiet.

"You and Kai," Jal began then stopped.

Aric sensed unease in the man. He remained staring into the night, giving him time to ask his questions.

"You and Kai, you have something between you. Am I right?" Jal finally got out. He looked away as if uncomfortable.

Aric smiled. "Yes. Kai is my life mate, and I am his. As he said, the amulet holder must be mated for life, and both must have the good of their clan, their tribe, in their hearts. We work as a team, but he is my leader."

"And what about Kai's woman, his wife?"

"There is a woman, Sable." He turned and looked into Jal's face. "She has born him young. We are a triad, but I am his first love."

"But, that means…" Jal stopped again.

"That would mean Kai has both a man and a woman who care for him. There are many among the tribes who pair up with the same sex. Is that not true among the horse *natsia*?"

Jal thought for a moment. "It's been known to happen, but not often. And never, that I know of, has a king shared his life with a man. There has always been a wife, someone to carry on the line."

"Ah, I see. It was a concern for Kai. Sable entered the picture and took care of that issue. But, that's not true of all the tribes." Aric told Jal what he knew about the leaders of the wolves and the bears. The young man listened with apparent interest. "The amulet will take care of who rules next, when the time comes."

"Do you think Brishen will be the one to hold the amulet?"

"We'll find out when Kai hands it to him. He'll know."

"He's proud. He'll rule. It's his destiny."

Aric looked at the man and sighed. Jal was so sure, so damn sure of this friend. Aric hoped it was true.

"And what of his wife?" Aric bit back a chuckle.

Jal jerked his head around and peered at Aric. "He doesn't have a wife. His father wanted him to take Tawnie, but that didn't happen."

"So, a possible triad," Aric murmured. "Interesting."

Jal got to his feet and paced around the dying fire. His brow was furrowed, and he bit his lower lip. "A triad," he said very quietly, as if trying it on for size.

Aric climbed to his feet and stretched his arms over his head. The yawn caught him by surprise.

"I've been a very poor host. You've been travelling all day, you've got to be exhausted."

"Yeah, I'm beat, but I did want to spend some time with you."

"And I thank you for your candid answers to my questions. You've given me much to think about."

"I'm glad I could be of help." Aric looked towards the tent Tawnie had shown the men to, and he took a few steps towards it. Over his shoulder, he called, "I'll see you tomorrow. Don't worry, I'm sure Brishen will be exactly what he's meant to be."

"I'm sure he will be. He's too proud not to be."

Aric strode to the large tent and entered.

Kai sat up and opened his arms.

Chapter Nine

Brishen awoke with a start. He groaned, softly, not wanting to wake anyone. He'd had a restless night, waking from nightmares where he kept losing something important, but he couldn't remember what it was. He'd just get back to sleep, and it would start up again.

He threw the bedding aside and climbed to his feet. A quick trip to the bathroom and he clambered back under the covers, shivering from the early morning chill. He snuggled down for a few minutes, hoping to drift off to sleep again, but it was useless. His mind raced with what the visitors had said, what they'd brought, and he wanted the day to get underway.

A face popped into the wagon, and the man smiled when he saw Brishen was awake. "I thought I heard you moving around in here."

"Yeah, come in and sit." Brishen pushed himself up and sat cross-legged facing the entrance, part of the covers draped over his shoulders, the rest bunched around his loins. "Nightmares kept me awake most of the night."

"Still thinking about your father? Or was it the visitors?" Dark-skinned Jal, dressed for the day, entered with two steaming mugs and sat at the foot of Brishen's bed. He handed Brishen a cup of the herbal tea that was the normal morning brew.

"Not sure, exactly." He blew on this tea then took a tentative sip, sighing at the small pleasure.

"Very odd." Jal cocked his head and seemed deep in thought.

"I'll be fine." Another sip gave Brishen a moment to gather his thoughts. "Tell me, what did you think of this Kai and his group?"

"I think they're very wise, but I also think they don't understand our ways."

"My thoughts exactly. I just hope I didn't act rashly in my speaking to them. The amulet, it belongs to the horse *natsia*, to the tribal leader." Thrusting out his chest, he added, "And even though I haven't been crowned the king yet, I will be soon."

Jal reached forward and laid his hand on Brishen's chest. "That is very true, Sire."

Brishen blinked. *Sire.* The word made his heart race and his blood roar. Yet, he had to be mindful of how he continued his talks with these other changelings. Something they'd said flashed into his thoughts. A life mate, the talisman could only belong to one who was partnered for life with someone who had the good of the *natsia* in his heart. Could that mean Tawnie?

His heart sank. He cared for her, but there was something missing. He gazed into Jal's eyes and knew he loved the man. Deep inside, he knew this was the mate he craved, no matter what his father had planned for him. Tawnie might be involved in his life, but she couldn't fulfil all of his desires.

"You look troubled, my leader." Jal's hand slid across Brishen's chest to his shoulder and stayed there. "I would be honoured if you'd share your worries with me."

"Perhaps having someone simply listen to me ramble will help me clear my head." Brishen took another sip of tea and leant back against one of the wooden supports. "Kai said the talisman would belong only to someone who is with a life mate. I have no mate. The thought of being with Tawnie doesn't seem enough for me. She's a fine woman and would bear strong sons for the *familiya,* but…"

"But?" urged Jal gently.

"Yes, but," Brishen said, then went on. "But, she's not the person I'm crazy in love with." Taking a deep breath, he decided he wasn't quite ready to go there and changed directions. "This stone with all the power. I want to be the one who takes it to the *natsia.* To each individual *familiya* and *vitsa.*

"I want so badly to be like this Cato, to travel the land and bring peace to the horses. I am the king. The ceremony is a mere formality, we all know that. The right should be mine." He stopped his rant before his anger appeared. What right did Kai or the others have to dictate to him, to anyone in his *natsia*?

"Brishen, you make me proud to know you. I sense your need to help the horse clans, and I'm sure the amulet will fall to you."

"But I have no life mate," he blurted out and felt the burden of his confession escape.

"Perhaps you do but just haven't seen it yet." Jal smiled and squeezed his shoulder. "Maybe the amulet knows these things."

"But to rule, I must be sure of progeny. I must have an heir."

"Perhaps, but leadership is more than simply being able to pass the title to your child. There have been kings who, though having children, wound up with none because of the continual warring."

Brishen nodded but still felt as if more needed to be said.

"After you and the others retired for the night, I sat and talked with Aric for a while. I learned much about the amulet and the leaders."

Brishen perked up. "Tell me! What did you learn?"

"The men who came, they are more than simply travelling companions. They are lovers. The cougar clan is ruled by a triad, Kai and Aric and Sable, the woman who apparently has born Kai young. The bears, they're a triad, too, but no females are involved. Yet, the amulet belongs to Tarek. The wolves, Cole and Zane, same story. They're lovers, and they have a woman who shares a tent with them. Men loving men and who are accepted as leaders."

Brishen didn't know what to say or how to feel. Jal, his friend, much more than a friend, was giving him an opening he'd only dreamed about. As king, he would no longer have to be concerned with what his father had wanted. But perhaps...

"Are you still with me, Sire?" Jal interrupted his thoughts.

"Yes, very much with you." Brishen reached forward and ran his fingers under Jal's chin. The temptation to draw him forward was nearly overpowering, but their guests awaited. And the amulet. "I need to dress. Would you see that Kai and the others are fed and ready to talk?"

Jal turned his head to the side and brushed his lips against Brishen's forearm, just above the wrist. "Yes, Sire. I will do whatever you ask."

"There's much more we have to talk about."

"Yes, there most certainly is. About us and the future and Tawnie's part in it. A lot of things."

"You make my head spin." Brishen smiled down at his lover. Yes, he could think it, could say it if and when he was asked. Jal was his lover. Nothing was going to change that.

He watched Jal leave then hurried to don his pants and tunic. There was much to do today and one person he needed to speak with before it all got started. Brishen left his wagon and went searching for his mother.

"She's gone to the river to wash clothing with Tasha and Seine," Annette, one of his cousins, informed him. "They'll be gone for a few hours."

Brishen smiled. His mother was old and still queen of the *natsia*, yet she insisted on doing her share of the daily chores. "Thank you." He touched pretty, raven-haired Annette's arm gently. She was one of the giggling females who'd ogled their visitors the night before. *She has no idea.* He chuckled when he thought that every one of the handsome, virile men in the group was partnered with another male. The knowledge made him happier than he'd been in weeks.

He glanced towards the centre of camp and saw the men eating breakfast with Tawnie and Jal. Brishen inhaled and blew the breath out slowly. He'd gone off a little half-cocked the last time they'd talked. He hoped he could convey his feelings in a more civilised manner today. He approached the group and smiled shyly. "Good morning. I trust you slept well?"

Everyone looked at him, but Kai was the first to speak. "Good morning, Brishen. Our accommodations were very acceptable, thank you. How about you? Did you rest easy last night?"

Brishen took a seat in the circle across from his dark lover and Tawnie. "No, not really. A million thoughts rushed in and out of my head all night long. There's so much I need to say to you, but I'm not sure I can convey how I really feel without coming across like an ass—which I've already done. I'm sorry about that."

Kai smiled. "No apology necessary. You've had a lot to absorb."

"More than you realise." He glanced quickly at Jal and Tawnie then back to Kai. "I'm going to be crowned the next king of the gypsy *natsia*. I've always known reuniting the *vitsas* would fall to my shoulders. I just never knew exactly *how* I could do it."

"It won't be easy." Kai eyed him levelly.

"If it were, my father would have done it years ago. He knew it would be a complicated procedure. I believe now he didn't have the tools he needed to begin the task. I think the amulet is the key to reuniting the *vitsas* and bringing the horse changeling *natsia* together again.

"And, with my father dead, the *vitsas* will revolt, one against the other, unless a strong leader takes a firm hand in leading them. The amulet is the key, but the man holding it must wield the power wisely, or all will be lost. I'm sure of that."

"I believe so, too." Kai nodded. "Cato believed it and made it happen."

"I can do this." Brishen tried to tamp down the eagerness in his voice. "With Cato as my guide, I can go to the *vitsas* and make them understand what needs to happen if the *natsia* is to survive." He kicked a clod of dirt with his toe and looked back up, hoping his eyes conveyed the fire burning in his belly. *"I'm going to be their king.* I want the *natsia* to succeed more than anything. To thrive and prosper."

Aric said quietly, "He has the good of the tribe in his heart."

Kai smiled. "That's exactly what I've been waiting to hear." He stood and removed something from his pocket.

Brishen's jaw gaped when he spotted the brilliant purple stone on the leather thong. His heart lurched. He wanted to hold the amulet and extended his hands.

"Wait." Kai held up one finger. He walked around the circle and paused in front of Tawnie. "Hold out your hands."

Shaking, she obliged.

Kai laid the talisman on her palm, and everyone stared at it.

"What's supposed to happen?" she whispered.

"We'll know it when we see it." Kai took the amulet back and stepped in front of Jal. "Hands."

Jal extended them and accepted the sparkling stone. "Does it talk or something?"

"In a manner." Kai scooped the charm up and went to stand in front of Brishen. "Your turn."

Brishen raised his palms and watched Kai lower the amulet into it. As soon at the stone touched his skin, it glowed with luminous energy. It grew warm, but not to the point of discomfort. *Just the opposite*. The talisman felt *very* comfortable in his hands.

"By the stars," Tawnie murmured, voice breathy with awe.

Jal rose and moved to stand next to Brishen, a wide grin splitting his face. They exchanged glances, and Jal said to the visitors proudly, "Guess that answers any questions you might have had."

Brishen's heart thumped wildly in his chest. Excitement and nervousness raced through him in equal quantities. "Opens up a whole new set of questions for me, though."

With a knowing smile, Kai gently removed the amulet from Brishen's hands. "Why don't I hang on to this a while longer? You and I have some talking to do. Shall we go for a walk?"

"Yes," Brishen agreed willingly. He touched Jal's arm. "I'll be back soon."

Jal nodded. One look from his dark eyes conveyed all the emotions Brishen hoped to see—desire, lust and love. *A great deal of love.*

Brishen thought his chest might burst from the incredible feelings suddenly welling within him. He turned towards Tawnie and touched her shoulder.

"You should eat breakfast," she told him.

He smiled at her nurturing. "I'm not hungry. But when I return, we need to talk. You, Jal and I need to have a heart-to-heart."

"Yes, Brishen." Her irises were wide, but other emotions shone through along with a fear he sensed in her. *Desire. Lust. Love.*

Brishen smiled. *Yep, all there.*

He walked to Kai's side and chose a path that would take them on a nice, long stroll through the woods. The cougar leader had much to tell him, and Brishen was ready to listen.

* * * *

It was nearly dark by the time Brishen directed Kai back to camp. He left his mentor with Aric by the fire and went in search of Tawnie and Jal. Before he got clear of the fire pit, his mother approached him, and Brishen paused to give her a hug.

"It's been a good day," he told her.

"I'm glad." Pesha reached up and patted his cheek. "I need to talk to you."

"I'm sorry I missed you this morning. You should take it easy. Let the others do more of the work. You've earned a rest."

She waved a hand. "I'll rest when I'm dead and gone. As long as I've still got two strong hands, I help with the chores. Listen to me, now." She cupped his face. "It's time for the crowning ceremony. You need to be recognised as king."

"But father—"

"Your father would be very proud of you. We've mourned long enough. Time to move forward, my son."

He nodded and swallowed. What he needed to tell her wouldn't be easy, but he had to do it. "Mother, there's something you must know. I've chosen Tawnie as my mate, but—"

"But you're not sure where that leaves Jal."

Brishen inhaled. "Jal. Yes. I care about him, Mother."

"I've always known that. Your father knew it, too. He thought Jal was a fine boy. The only concerns Shandor had were for you. It's not always easy being different, even when you're a king."

He grinned. "On the contrary, I find that makes it very easy. As king, I can do what I want."

Her wrinkled face scowled. "Perhaps. It might be easy here, where we know and love you. When you go out into the world, talking to *Bandoleers* of the other *vitsas*, your position might not be so comfortable."

Brishen thought about the men he'd met in the past few days—Kai, Aric, Cole and Zane—strong, powerful men who garnered respect because they deserved it. He felt confident he could lead in much the same manner and was aching to try. "I can do this, Mother."

She gazed at him for a moment then stepped back and nodded. "I believe you can. Always remember how proud your father was of you. How proud I am. You are Brishen, son of Shandor. And you will be King of the Gypsies."

"I love you, old woman." He pecked the side of her face.

She patted him one last time. "Don't forget, we expect heirs."

"I'll never forget." The words reminded him where he'd been going in the first place. *To find Jal and Tawnie.* He wasn't sure where they'd be but started by looking for them in his wagon.

They were curled up in separate corners of his bed, sipping tea. "Brishen!" Tawnie's face lit up when she spotted him. "You were gone so long. We were worried."

He crawled between them and flopped onto his back. "It was an incredible day. Kai told me so much. Showed me so much."

A hint of jealousy tinged Jal's voice. "You sound enamoured with the cougar man. Remember, he's a wild beast, totally different from us."

"I know." Brishen tucked his hands under his head, staring at the top of the wagon as he spoke. "We shifted into animals this afternoon and ran and ran. We rested by the river, and while I dined on wild greens, he stalked and killed a rabbit. It was bloody and gory—and simply amazing."

"Yuck!" Tawnie shuddered. "I'm so glad horses aren't hunters. I couldn't stand the blood."

Brishen chuckled. The equine diet was primarily vegetarian, but every now and then the gypsies added some meat to a stew. He couldn't imagine Tawnie as a huntress but knew he wouldn't want her any other way. "Well, as I said, I found it fascinating. I'm glad I was able to spend time with Kai today. I'm even happier to be home with the two of you. We need to talk."

"What is it?" Apprehension clouded Tawnie's face.

It took Brishen a moment to realise she had no idea what he'd been planning. Although he'd settled things in his mind, Tawnie was clearly still unsure of where she was in his scheme of things. He wanted to let her off the hook immediately.

"I love you," he blurted out. "I want to be with you and have a whole herd of foals. But I need to tell you, I love Jal, too." He cast a quick glance at the man who'd captured his heart.

Jal's eyes were brimming with emotions that looked a lot like love and pride.

Tawnie opened her mouth to speak, but Brishen kept talking, words spilling out in a rush. "I know our situation isn't normal, but if the last couple of days have shown me anything, it's that there are lots of different kinds of normal. You have to understand, my feelings go beyond the wishes of my father. Please believe me, I've given this a great deal of consideration. I know exactly what I want."

"Jal," she said simply. "You want Jal."

"I can't deny it. Being with Jal is something I've wanted for too long. I won't ignore that side of my heart any longer. But when I think about the both of you, together, *being with both of you,* that's when I truly feel complete. I don't know, maybe it's too crazy to explain." He closed his eyes, suddenly feeling foolish.

Soft fingertips brushed his arm, and he opened his eyes to look into Tawnie's.

"It's not that crazy," she told him. "Jal and I had it figured out a long time before you did. It seems very logical for three people who are so closely connected to share one romance."

Brishen blinked. He'd stewed over this decision for what seemed like forever. He could hardly believe Tawnie suggested it so easily. "You'd be willing to do that?"

Jal moved closer, placing his hand on Brishen's other arm. "It's what we were hoping for."

Heart aflutter, all Brishen could think about was what might go wrong. Jealousies, bickering... Things that might happen in a relationship with two people could be intensified with a third person thrown into the mix. He was about to voice more concerns when he felt tugging at the waistband of his trousers. "Wha—"

"Shhh."

Jal leaned over him, their mouths so close Brishen felt his warm breath.

"No more 'what ifs'. Lie still and let us love you." Jal pressed his lips to Brishen's.

There was little time to object, not that he intended to. Tawnie had unfastened his jeans and dragged them down over his hips. His erection sprang to life, aided by her soft, wet kisses.

"Please," he murmured when Jal allowed him time for a breath.

Dark eyes held their gaze steadily on his. Brishen saw a smile play over Jal's lips.

"Please what, lover?" Jal murmured seductively.

Any hope of rational thought flew from Brishen's mind. *No more thinking, no more talking.* He ached to feel every caress the two sets of hands offered. Longed to taste the kisses being plied on him so sweetly. "Please, more."

Jal's mouth captured his again. Jal's tongue drove deep, exploring the ridges of Brishen's teeth in exacting detail.

Brishen's head spun. The intensity of the two mouths on him was unbelievable. Jal's kisses left him giddy, and the thorough tongue-lashing Tawnie lavished on his cock caused him to clench his ass cheeks to keep from spewing.

With a smooth shift of bodies, Jal's rampant erection replaced the tongue in Brishen's mouth.

Tamping down momentary surprise, Brishen sucked it eagerly, savouring the salty pre-cum that oozed down his throat. So focused on the delectable treat in front of him, he lost track of Tawnie until she climbed on top and impaled herself on his shaft.

The hard thrust caused his eyes to roll back in his head. Brishen groaned, sure he'd spill his load now. He tried to think about anything besides the two sexy creatures ravishing him but had no luck. His balls drew up, and he felt the first twinges of what was sure to be an earth-shattering orgasm.

"Oh, yes! Yes!" Tawnie cried, pummelling herself.

Jal thrust his cock in and out of Brishen's mouth with vigour. His voice was throaty as he muttered, "Fuck, yeah. Damn, this is hot."

Brishen struggled to get a glimpse of Tawnie around Jal's sweat-slicked body. He finally saw the pale-haired beauty, eagerly massaging her breasts, face contorted in ecstasy as she rode Brishen to her own release. It was all he needed to send him spiralling into a climax so intense that, for several minutes, he couldn't tell that the groaning sound filling the wagon came from him.

Tawnie's cunt clenched around him as she came. Brishen heard her wails and moans but couldn't focus—Jal was filling his mouth with warm, musky cream. He swallowed what he could but finally gave up and allowed the overflow to drip down his chin.

He started to protest when the two warm bodies left his, but relaxed as each of his lovers curled into one of his arms, nestling against his chest. Brishen kissed Tawnie on the forehead then turned and did the same to Jal. He wanted to tell them how much the encounter had meant to him, but emotion filled his head, and he couldn't form the words.

Jal tossed one leg over Brishen and reached out to rub Tawnie's arm. She did the same with her leg, until she and Jal were knee to knee. They nudged each other affectionately.

"Fuck," Jal murmured.

"Oh, yeah." Tawnie sighed then yawned. She snuggled closer to Brishen and closed her eyes.

"Uh huh," Brishen whispered. He realised, at that moment, he didn't need to find the words. Both his lovers knew exactly how he felt, and they felt the same way.

Epilogue

Amazed, Brishen watched the crowd of people gathered to watch his crowning ceremony and wedding. Once the news had spread, two other *vitsas* came to join the festivities. He'd spoken with their *Bandoleers* and was pleased to learn they were as ready for peace as his *familya*. The older leaders warned that everyone in the territory might not be as accepting of the new, young king, but Brishen was elated. Three *vitsas* banded together on this day. It was a start.

He stood in the clearing by the campfire with the gypsies and *gajes* circled around him. His mother, in her role as Gypsy Queen, had prepared a special drink from a secret initiation recipe. She carried the cup into the crowd so it could be touched by each gypsy present. Brishen heard Jal in the front row describing the ceremony to Kai, Aric, Cole and Zane.

"After everyone has touched the cup, Brishen will drink from it. Tradition suggests that if he's worthy of being king, his blood will change to royal blood, and he'll have powerful visions."

"And if he's not worthy?" Aric asked.

Jal shrugged. "If he's unworthy or false-hearted, he'll fall into convulsions and die."

Brishen bit back a grin. He fully expected to be deemed worthy.

The Queen approached him with the cup. "Drink, my son."

He took the old, silver chalice and sipped from it. The liquid was bitter but not bad, and he tossed the last of it back.

The crowd held its collective breath as they watched for his reaction.

Brishen lowered the cup, smiled then raised it high as a symbol of victory.

A roar of approval rang out. Cheers of, "Hail, Brishen, King of the Gypsies!" sounded with the rumble of applause. Women from his *familya* appeared, layering him in the brightly coloured scarves of the tribe.

"No crown?" Aric asked Jal.

"No crown," Jal repeated. "We aren't that gauche."

Brishen glanced down at the layers of garish scarves around his neck and grinned.

"Okay," Jal relented. "We're slightly gauche. But these serve another purpose, as well."

Two of Brishen's cousins, Tasha and Annette, brought Jal and Tawnie out of the crowd and stood them next to the king.

"Hello," he smiled at them.

"Hello, King," Tawnie replied.

"Sire," Jal acknowledged.

Brishen's heart raced. The events of the day were already overwhelming, yet they were about to get better.

His mother stood before them with two men in brightly coloured robes. "Since I'm no longer the queen, the binding ceremony will be performed by the two *Bandoleers* with us today." Pesha kissed Brishen's cheek and pulled two of the scarves from around his neck. She handed them to the *Bandoleers* and stepped back.

Both men stepped forward, and one spoke. "Extend your hands, please."

Brishen, Jal and Tawnie held out their hands and watched as the men lashed them together.

"The handfasting ceremony binds you together in matrimony. Each participant will now make a promise about what he or she brings to the marriage."

His heart near bursting, Brishen looked back and forth from the eyes of Jal to Tawnie. "I guess I'll go first. I promise to be here and support each of you through good times and bad. I'll be the best partner and provider I can be, and I'll love you both until the day I die."

Jal nodded to Tawnie, and she spoke next. "I vow to nurture each of you to the best of my ability, and to welcome foals into our *familiya* with that same spirit. I'll be here for you when you need me, and I will always keep our home filled with love."

Brishen smiled at her, and they both looked at Jal.

Jal blinked a few times rapidly, as if he didn't know what to say. They all chuckled, and he spoke. "My King and My Queen, I shall be at your service, day or night. Whenever you need me, call." His eyebrows wagged lewdly. "Seriously, as your mate, I'll be your protector, your champion, your advisor in all things. And I'm looking forward to every minute of it, because I love you both very much."

The *Bandoleers* unfastened the scarves from around their hands. Annette and Tasha came forward, this time wrapping scarves around the three of them as they joined in a group hug. The roar of the crowd was deafening.

Brishen took the opportunity to kiss each of his mates and hugged them tight as Jal and Tawnie kissed. "I love you!" he called over the din.

"We love you, too." Tawnie cupped his face. "And we plan to prove it once this party is over."

Jal groaned. "I've heard the dancing and drinking at these wedding parties sometimes goes on all night long."

"Maybe for them." Brishen nodded towards the crowd. "We'll stay long enough to celebrate, get a little buzz on, then I'm afraid we're going to have to quietly slip off. I have a different type of dancing in mind, and it doesn't require a crowd."

"Just three," Tawnie added.

"Definitely three." Brishen hugged them tightly one more time.

They joined the wedding party, where they were immediately plied with food and drink. When he came up for air, Brishen noticed Kai and his group standing off to the side, appearing as if they were ready to leave. He set his plate aside and went to speak with them.

"Did you get something to eat?"

"We did, and now we have to go." Kai shouldered his pack. "We want to start our return trek before it gets any later. We've all been gone from home long enough. And we did promise Tarek we'd stop and let him know how things worked out here."

"I'm sorry I didn't get to meet him."

Kai fingered the amulet around his neck. "His tribe had problems with one of the local hunters. It's been resolved, all is well. Perhaps you'll meet him another time."

Brishen eyed the talisman and Kai with awe. He pulled the purple amulet from under his shirt and said, "I hope one day I'm as in tune with this as you are with yours."

"You will be." Kai glanced around at the crowd of people. "This is a very good start, right here. I have no doubts, before long you'll be ruling the entire horse changeling *natsia* with a firm hand and a good heart."

Aric nodded. "Give it time, Brishen. You'll do fine."

"Thanks to you. All of you." Brishen made eye contact with each of the men and tried to convey his sincere appreciation.

"Good luck," Cole said as he and Zane hefted their packs. "We're just over the mountain about a half day's journey if you ever need anything."

Brishen nodded, and the four travellers turned, making their way into the forest. Just as they reached the cover of trees, they shifted, morphing into their animal forms. He watched the two cougars and two wolves sprint off into the distance until they were out of sight.

Jal and Tawnie approached him on either side. "Everything all right?" Jal nudged Brishen's shoulder with his own.

With one last look towards the woods and the strangers who had changed his life, Brishen faced his mates and slipped an arm around each of their waists. "Everything is wonderful. We have so much to look forward to, so much to do. But for tonight, let's have one more glass of wine then move this party to our wagon, shall we?"

Tawnie and Jal smiled and nodded their agreement. They strolled back to their camp, their *familya* and their future.

About the Authors

Jenna Byrnes

Jenna Byrnes could use more cabinet space and more hours in a day. She'd fill the kitchen with gadgets her husband purchases off TV and let him cook for her to his heart's content. She'd breeze through the days adding hours of sleep, and more time for writing the hot, erotic romance she loves to read.

Jenna thinks everyone deserves a happy ending, and loves to provide as many of those as possible to her gay, lesbian and hetero characters. Her favourite quote, from a pro-gay billboard, is "Be careful who you hate. It may be someone you love."

Jude Mason

Jude's imagination frequently leads her astray and she eagerly follows while trying to keep out of trouble, or at least, not get caught. For those of you who know her, you'll know that's not always easy. A picture, a smell, an unexpected glimpse of flesh, or a load of soil in the back of a pick-up, are all fodder for her writing. Her male characters run the gamut from the dominant male ruling his women with an iron fist, to a simpering purple-clad boy-toy whose only desire is to please. As diverse and as richly depicted, her women find themselves in a myriad of exotic and erotic situations.

Jenna and Jude love to hear from readers. You can find their contact information, website details and author profile pages at http://www.total-e-bound.com

Total-E-Bound Publishing

www.total-e-bound.com

Take a look at our exciting range of literagasmic™
erotic romance titles and discover pure quality
at Total-E-Bound.

Lightning Source UK Ltd.
Milton Keynes UK
UKOW051054030212

186595UK00001B/131/P